WALKER

Bowen Boys
Book 1

SECOND EDITION

By

KATHI S. BARTON

World Castle Publishing, LLC

WCP

World Castle Publishing

Pensacola, Florida

ISBN: 9781939865229

First Edition World Castle Publishing April 10, 2013

Second Edition World Castle Publishing August 19, 2013

http://www.worldcastlepublishing.com

Cover: Karen Fuller

Photos: Shutterstock, iStock

Editor: Eric Johnston

CHAPTER ONE

Lynne ran. Not that she figured she could outrun them, but she had to try. And if she could get far enough in front of them so that she could turn the tide on them, then she'd do it. She no longer looked behind her, because every time she did, they seemed nearly ready to grab her. Taking a small stumble had cost her precious seconds, but she recovered and kept running. Soon, they'd have her anyway, but she wouldn't go easily.

Tree limbs tore at her skin. There were cuts on her legs and arms that she knew she'd feel if she ever got to sit down. Her face screamed in pain. The last branch that had scratched her cut deeply, and the blood flowed down her chin, but it was only another wound on her already battered face where they had punched and slapped at her. Her arm was broken. But still, she ran.

Three days ago—had it only been that short of a time span since she'd been in her own bed? The alarm to the windows hadn't sounded, and even the ones to her bedroom door hadn't awakened her. She'd been sleeping soundly when, without warning, there was a rag over her mouth and she'd breathed in the first whiff of chloroform.

The first pain that ripped into her shoulder nearly took her down and brought her from her memories. The second one in her thigh made her fall. She had to get up. She could hear them laughing behind her. There was blood pouring from her leg, and she could only imagine what her shoulder was doing.

Getting up, she was off again, limping. She had just made it to the trees when pain ripped through her calf. Pain throbbed as hard as her heart was beating. She could barely breathe through it. Leaning against a tree to get her bearings, she heard one of the men speak close beside her. She figured they were only about ten feet from her now.

"Come out, come out, wherever you are. Come on, McCray, it's not any fun when you don't give us a sporting chance. You come out and run again and we'll slow down running after you." He laughed, and she knew his brother was close, as well. "Tommy here said he'd give you a ten-minute head start. That's more than you deserve after what you've done to us."

She felt the tears mix with the blood on her face. She hated tears more than she hated these men. All she'd done was call the police on the pricks. She thought they should obey the law of not stealing from your neighbor. They'd broken into her home four or five days ago and kidnapped her, but she was sure as she was standing there that they'd had help. Tommy and Jay Ingram were the meanest men she'd ever encountered, but they were also the stupidest. And today, when they'd told her their plan, she'd never dreamed they were serious.

She was to be their prey, and they'd hunt her like an animal. If she gave them a good time, they wouldn't rape her. If she didn't play fair, then they'd fuck her over and over until she was dead, then leave her where she lay to let the animals have a feast on her dead body.

"Yeah, you come on out and show yourself to us and I'll give you those ten minutes that Jay said I would." They snickered like five-year-olds. "I got me a stopwatch all ready for you."

Someone broke a stick right where she was standing and she nearly bolted. But at the last second she froze. Right in front of her was the biggest cat she'd ever seen. She didn't even know that panthers lived in that part of the world.

He was staring at her with the darkest, most intelligent eyes she'd ever seen. And he wasn't moving. She was sure that if she moved, he would take her down and have her for dinner. Right now, she didn't know if having a big cat chew her up would be preferable to being raped repeatedly and then murdered. When another branch broke, she looked to her left and saw that Jay was almost close enough to touch.

The cat was looking between the man, about two feet away from her, and back at her. She didn't, for whatever reason, want the panther hurt, so she leaned down slowly, praying that her knees wouldn't pop, and picked up a small rock. She showed it to him and was sure he nodded at her.

Lynne was hurting and couldn't see well, but tried to think where would be the best place to throw it. Looking as far to the left of her as she could without giving away her position, she held her breath and threw it as hard as she could. When it hit a tree near her, about ten feet away, she nearly cried out in frustration, but when the men took off in that direction, she bolted to the other. She'd have to live to fight another day.

She stumbled twice…once when the cat stood up, then again when the pain gripped her so tightly it nearly knocked her over. Falling to the ground, she turned to see the brothers coming at her, and they looked pleased. She didn't have it in her to fight now…she was all done in.

"That wasn't very nice, Lynne. We played fair and now you—" The big cat lunged at Jay and took him down. The shot that rang out made her think that she'd been hit again, but she saw that Tommy had the gun pointed at his brother and the cat. Struggling to stand, she hoped the cat ate them and silently thanked him for his help.

Another shot rang out and she heard a scream. Shuddering and still moving slowly forward, she tried not to think about the cat and how he'd saved her life. She might make it if she didn't bleed to death first.

Twice she had to stop to lean against a tree. When she grew too weak to move, she sat down. Gathering as many leaves as she could find on the earthy floor, she covered herself and leaned gently against the tree behind her. Her back screamed at the pain, but she was to the point she couldn't go on. Closing her eyes, she thought that dying right there would be the best solution to her weakness. Either she'd be too weak when they found her and she wouldn't care, or the big cat or one like him would come find her and eat her. Again, she probably wouldn't care.

~~~

Corrine reached for her son. The old fool just lay there, staring up at her. She looked at her mate and wanted to kick him in the head. The darned old fool. When Khan answered her, she wanted to cry. He always sounded so distrustful.

"You have to come to the west wood. You're not going to believe this. Your father has been shot." She felt his immediate concern, and she continued. *"He's going to be fine, more's the pity. What possessed him to take on a man with a gun? Could have been the girl, but I don't know. I would say it was the poor thing. All beat up like that."*
~~~

"Someone beat Dad? When? Where? What girl are you talking about? I'm coming, and I'm bringing the rest with me." She told him to bring the truck. He would need to load the old buzzard in it. *"Can he shift, Mom? Is he hurt badly?"*

"No. He'll be fine. He and I were out exploring when we came up on this noise." She looked off in the direction that the girl had gone, knowing that she wouldn't have gotten far. *"Tell Walker to come to me. I want him to see if he can find the girl before...she might already be dead, the poor thing."*

"Mom, we don't need to find a girl. And I'm assuming you mean a human girl. Let her die if that's what is necessary. She shouldn't have been on—"

"Listen to me, young man. You will stop that train of bull hockey right now. I will not have a young woman die on this property if there is something this old woman and you can do to fix it." She looked at her mate again. *"You stay home if you don't want to help, but send Walker. Now."*

Corrine wasn't pack leader any longer, but she was still Khan's mother and he would listen to her or she'd take a paddle to his hide. She didn't care how much larger he was than her, he'd darned well listen to her. Kneeling down next to George, she ran her finger down his cheek and smacked him. Darned old fool.

Walker showed up first. His long panther was sleek with sweat from getting to her so quickly. She waited for him to check out his dad before she told him what she needed. He was a good boy, and unlike his older brother, Walker didn't hate everyone that wasn't like them.

"She was leaning against that tree. There's enough blood on it for you to scent her." He stood up against the tree and buried his nose in the bark. When he turned to look at her, he had a very strange expression on his face before he turned back to the tree and licked the blood. "She went that way, but

I'm pretty sure she didn't get far. I know she's been shot at least twice, and her face…." She wiped at the tear. "Walker, the men who shot your dad were intent on killing her or worse. I believe they beat her pretty badly as well."

Walker dropped to his four paws and took off, but not before he leaned against her and whimpered. She assured him that she would be all right until the others got there and sent him on his way. She had no idea where the girl or the men who had been chasing her had come from, but they had been on family land, their land. Corrine sat next to George and waited for the cavalry to show up.

The first person to get out of the big truck was Dylan, the bad boy of the family, yet so calm. He was one of her middle children and the most laid back of all her sons. He walked over to his dad and felt his pulse much the same way she had every two minutes since she'd shifted to care for the old man.

Khan and Reed, the oldest at thirty-six and the baby at twenty-six, rolled out next, both nearly vibrating with anger. Marc just stood back and smiled. He always was one to give others a chance to settle things before he took over. Khan, she had an idea why he was upset, but Reed she didn't. Before she could ask, he looked at Khan and picked up the argument that had apparently been going on for some time.

"And what does it matter to you one bit if I move out on my own? Maybe if I did, you'd quit breathing down my neck all the time. I went to college like you made me. I thought you'd back—"

"When you get settled in a job, maybe. You want to end up in a dead-end job without any kind of future? I say no. You'll do what I tell you, or so help me—"

"Enough." Corrine looked at George and nearly wept with happiness. But he looked mad enough to tear into both them and the men who had shot him. Then his voice thundered again. “That’s quite enough out of both of you. You’re upsetting your mother. Now, help me up. Where’s that girl?”

“I sent Walker after her. She’s hurt pretty badly.” She let George lean on her as they made their way to the truck. One of the boys, she noticed, had put a single mattress in the back for him. “Walker will be able to track her with all that blood. And he’s the best suited to find her. He’s supposed to let me know when he does.”

“Those damned men. What the hell were they thinking running her down like they were?” He looked up at Khan when he growled. “What you got to say, boy? Spill it.”

“She’s human. The better question is what the hell was she doing on our property with them? We don’t need their kind around here.”

“She wasn’t with them. She was being run down by them. That one had already shot her a couple of times, and if’n you had seen her face and body you’d know that you’re barking up the wrong tree.” George lay down on the mattress after being lifted up into the bed. “Wouldn’t be right of us not to help her. She probably saved my hide too. Nearly pissed myself when she showed me that rock.”

Corrine had no idea what he was talking about, but didn’t say anything. The old fool was out of his mind. She started to climb up in the bed with him when Khan pulled her back down.

“You ride inside and I’ll stay with him. My mom won’t be riding in the back like that.”

She wanted to smack him and hug him.

“Please.”

“All right, but you let me know at the first sign of trouble.” She looked at George and felt her heart twist a little, remembering him falling like he had. "He's stubborn, but I love him."

"Of course you—" Khan stopped and looked out toward where she'd sent Walker. "He's found her. He said she's weak and has lost a great deal of blood. He said he wants to treat her at the house."

She waited for what she knew was coming. When he didn't, she did for him. "And you told him no."

"We don't need her kind sniffing around where we live. For all we know, she might have done this so she could get close to us to expose us."

Corrine didn't say anything, but hugged him to her. If she thought she could get away with it, she'd hunt down that woman who had hurt her son and rip her throat out. But this one needed their help now. The door closed with a hard snap, and she looked over at Dylan, who was driving. His raised brow said a great deal, but she didn't give him what he wanted. She didn't have any answers either.

"Khan said your brother found the girl. Go that way." She pointed to where Walker was. "We'll put her beside your dad if we have to. But we're not leaving her out here in the woods to die alone."

Dylan nodded and started the truck. Reed sat beside her and stared out the window. He was still mad, and she wanted to comfort him, but knew he'd not be happy with her if she did. Even though he was her baby, he was a grown man.

It took them ten minutes to get to where Walker was. He was a man now, having shed his panther. But he didn't look any less dangerous. She watched him pace as they got closer and wondered where the girl was. When they pulled up beside the tree where he was, she got out and looked at him. He was more than a little upset.

"They beat her with what appears to be a whip. She's been shot three times, one in the shoulder, the left thigh, and once in the right calf. How she got this far is beyond me." He moved from the tree, and Corrine saw her then. He'd covered her with his flannel shirt. "Her heart rate is slow, but she's strong. Healthy. If we take her to the hospital, we're going to have to explain what—"

"We *are* taking her to the hospital. That's final. I don't want anyone coming around here and asking questions we don't have answers for."

Before she could say anything to Khan, his father did.

"Walker, put her in here. Right here beside me. We'll take her to our house and help her there." No one moved. "*Walker*. Do what I tell you. Khan, move out of the way. You don't want to help, that's fine, but you aren't going to be a hindrance either."

Corrine moved toward the girl with Reed. They were going to do it even if no one else did. As soon as she saw her, though, she couldn't move. The girl looked close to dying.

"They did her wrong. I didn't see any signs of rape, but they hurt her. She smells like them."

She looked over at her son when he stood beside her.

"I'm going to find them, and when I do, I'm going to kill them slowly for what they did to her."

Corrine looked back at the girl and wiped away her tears. "Your dad said she saved his life. That she did something to distract them from finding him so they could both run."

Walker nodded. "I want you to take Dad back to the house and you bring the truck back, please. Then you and I will load her up and take her to the house."

His voice was low, lower than it had been when he was telling her what he'd found out about her not being raped. She looked at him, wondering why he thought she'd leave his dad over coming out to help this poor little girl. When it occurred to her she could only stare at him with her mouth open.

"Yeah. I didn't see that one coming either. She can't ride with Dad and I don't want to hurt Reed when he helps me lift her." He put his arm around her and held her close to whisper the rest. "I will hurt him and you know it. Can you please help me with this?"

"Yes. I'll take your…can I at least tell your father?" He nodded, then shook his head. "Walker?"

"I can't bring her into this. You have to know that. She's a human and we're not even close to being…." He glanced at her, then away. "Khan will wish her dead. I can't have my family torn apart because I suddenly find myself with a mate."

Corrine looked at Khan, who seemed to be ready to murder someone, anyone who dared to speak to him. She looked back at Walker and knew that he might be able to hold his own with his brother, but Khan was their leader now and as such would be naturally stronger than his younger brother. She looked back at the girl, who had no idea how much trouble she'd caused by simply being a victim. "I'll stay here with her, and Dylan will bring the truck back. We'll take her to the hospital and leave her there." He started to protest, but she cut him off. "You don't want her, then you will not make yourself nuts with her being here. I've spoken, and you're going to obey."

She sat on the ground next to the girl and held her hand. She was cold, but her pulse, while slow, was strong. Corrine didn't know what to do about her being Walker's mate. She could see his point about Khan, but she doubted that he'd harm her knowing what she was to his brother. However, she would make it difficult. When the truck pulled away, she looked at her second son and hurt for him, then looked back at the girl.

"You poor thing. So much love could be yours but for the hatred of another of your kind. She hurt his brother and now…." She looked at Walker again. "And now you're going to be hurt more, I think. Or maybe you'll be the one to bring him around."

Twenty minutes later, the truck pulled up. This time there was only Dylan in it; the other had apparently stayed behind. The mattress was covered this time, and there was a medical kit beside it. Along with a few blankets, there was some bottled water and some of her old rags.

Corrine watched as Walker lifted the girl and put her gently in the back of the truck. He stiffened when she cried out, and her heart hurt for them both. As soon as she was lifted into the bed beside the girl, they were off. She told Dylan to take them to the emergency room. Walker told him to take her to his house. Dylan nodded and started the engine. Corrine wondered where they would end up. She wasn't the least bit surprised to see that they were headed to the house. Things were about to get interesting for them all. Walker was in for the time of his life. She only hoped that the girl beside her could fix it.

CHAPTER TWO

Lynne felt as if she was coming up for air when she woke with a rush. She could hear her heart pounding in her ears, fearing the unknown and that the Ingram boys had found her after all. She really had hoped that the panther would have found her, knowing that he would have made her death quick. Before she could linger on that thought, she heard a noise and looked toward it.

"Hello, dear. How are you today?" Lynne watched the woman approach what she now realized was a bed. "I know you're probably hurting very badly, but you've been here for several days and I wanted to make sure your family knew you were all right. Can you tell me who you are?"

She did hurt and was hurting more by the second. As parts of her body began to scream at her, she looked around the room the best she could. It didn't look like anything that the Ingram's might live in. This place was much nicer and a great deal cleaner. Lynne tried to focus on the woman's face and got the impression of dark but graying hair and a friendly face. It took her two tries to answer her.

"There's no one." She closed her eyes against the overwhelming pain. "Not even a cat." The laughter from the woman startled her, and she peered at her through what felt like sand and fuzz.

"No, you don't own a cat. We would have known that right away." She came closer, sat down on a chair that Lynne had just noticed, and took her hand. "You're going to be fine, my dear. You should try to rest again. Next time you wake up, I'll have you some broth made."

Lynne closed her eyes and started to drift again when she suddenly remembered something. "Don't let them hurt that cat. He wasn't hurting anyone. And please don't give me back to them. I don't want to die by their hand. They'll make me suffer."

"They won't get to come near you again. You just rest, and the cat? He's just fine too. A little on the ornery side, but going to be just fine."

Lynne heard her, but didn't think she'd heard her correctly. She couldn't hold her eyes open any longer and let herself drift away. She knew fleetingly that something was taking away the pain, but didn't have time to think about it before she was in a black void.

The room was bright with light when she woke the next time…or at least the time that she was awake for more than a few seconds. She'd been laying there thinking about how much she hurt and wondering where she was when a noise sounded close to her. Opening one eye, she saw an older man sitting in the chair that had been occupied by the woman from before.

Lynne had seen her sometimes when she'd wake, screaming in pain. She'd not meant to do that, but her own voice was what had awakened her. The woman had comforted her, soothing her with softly spoken words. Lynne had no idea what they were, but had slipped away when she'd taken her arm. Lynne knew she was giving her something for pain and whatever it was made her feel very good. The man clearing his throat had her looking at him.

"You're safe here. My mate and I have been caring for you for ten days now. I don't know how long those men had you, but you are safe here with us." His voice seemed to rumble from his chest. "Can you tell me who you are?"

"Lynne." She swallowed to try again. "Caitlynne McCray. But I go by Lynne. Where am I?" She hurt, but not as badly as she had, and she began to take inventory of her body. The man leaned forward and picked up a glass with a straw hanging out of it. He offered it to her, and she turned her head. He didn't say anything as he put it back on the bedside table.

"I'm George Bowen, and my wife, who's been caring for you mostly, is Corrine Bowen. You're in our son's home…my second son's home. Walker has been your doctor." He leaned back in the chair and smiled. "You're very lucky that we found you when we did. Those men meant to harm you."

They had. But she didn't say anything. She needed to get out of there and find the pricks so she could use her own kind of punishment on them. She was up to her thigh when she felt the shooting pain there. He must have noticed her whimper a little.

"He removed the bullets. There were three altogether. And the lashes on your back are healing nicely. He had to stitch up a few of them, but he said you'd not have too much in the way of scarring." He picked up a small cell phone when it rang and spoke quickly to someone on the other end. "Yes, she's awake now. No, I don't believe she'll be able to do that just yet. I know what you said, Khan, but this isn't your house and he can let whomever he wants, whenever he wants, stay here. You do that."

He hung up the phone, and she tried to sit up. He stood up, but didn't come to her aid. Just as well; he might be old, but she was pretty sure he could take her if he wanted. By the time she was sitting up, she was covered in sweat and in so much pain that she thought she was going to be sick with it. The door opening had them both looking toward it.

The man standing there was more than big, he was fucking huge. When he stalked toward the bed, she cowered. When he didn't move any closer, she looked at him.

"I won't harm you."

She shivered at the sound of his voice and pulled the cover up over her shoulders. Even that small movement wore her out.

"I was only going to check on you before I went to the hospital to see to another patient."

"She only just woke up, Walker. Come and introduce yourself to Caitlynne McCray. Oh, she wants to be called Lynne." The younger man looked at the older one and seemed to glare. Lynne was startled by his bark of laughter. "You don't scare me with that look, young man. I'm your father. Come here and speak to her. I'm going to tell your mother that she's awake."

George got up and went to the door, but stopped long enough to shove the younger man toward her. She might have thought it was funny if she wasn't terrified of him. He didn't speak as he settled into the empty chair. Then, when he reached for her hand, she snatched it back.

"I need to feel your pulse. Please." She put out her arm and was embarrassed to see it tremble. He pushed her gently back on the bed and she had to let him. She was in no shape to fight him. "It's a little fast, but that could be because you're angry."

This time when she snatched her hand back she put it under the covers. She was already getting tired and wanted him to say whatever it was he wanted, then to go away. She looked around the room for her clothes. When he chuckled, she looked back at him.

"You're in no shape to leave just yet, if that's what you're thinking. The bullets that entered your leg were clean shots, but the wounds will need to be babied for a few more days. The one in your shoulder is doing well too, but again, will need to be kept still so that you don't tear out the stitches. Who was it that was chasing you?"

His change of subject startled her, but she knew better than to simply answer because he asked. She'd been trained to be on the alert to such ploys. She pulled the blanket back to see what sort of injuries she had. He laughed again, but she ignored him this time.

"When can I walk on it?" She glanced at the door again and wondered how much energy it would take to make it there. "I have places I need…. Why aren't I at a hospital?"

"I decided that it would be safer for all of us if you remained here. And you won't be able to leave until I say so."

She raised a brow at him. His laughing at her was getting on her nerves. She lay back on the bed and closed her eyes.

~~~

Walker watched her until she fell asleep. He knew she had to be hurting, but didn't give her anything for the pain. She'd be just stubborn enough to get out of bed and do some serious damage to his work before she fell again. He reached up and brushed a lock of her hair from her face.

When she'd first been brought to the house his mother had helped him clean her up. Her face had taken a beating, and the rest of her body hadn't fared much better. While there were no broken ribs, she was badly bruised, and he had been
~~~

able to make out boot print bruising on her. Her legs were covered in long, wide scratches, probably from her run, and her arms, too, were covered in scrapes as well as numerous cuts. He looked at the marks on her wrists again, and his anger returned.

She'd been beaten; her back told him that story. A whip had been used, and if he didn't miss his guess, he'd say a belt as well, the buckle end on her tender skin. He'd had to stitch up quite a few of them, two cuts along her breasts, especially.

Her face had intrigued him. Neither he nor his mom had been able to tell anything about her looks. Her face had been swollen, her eyes too. The left eye had been hurt so badly that blood had filled it until recently. Now he could see that they were a lovely shade of blue.

And lovely she was…a small, pert nose, high cheekbones, as well as full, lush lips that he wanted so desperately to kiss. The swelling had gone down considerably, and in its place was a woman he could look at, and wanted to for the rest of his life. He leaned back in the chair and thought about her and the relationship that could never be. Everything about her made him want to strip down and crawl into bed with her and never leave.

Khan hadn't actually forbidden it, but he had been very vocal in that he didn't want her there. He could understand him to a point, and his brother, oldest of them all, was the new leader. But neither Khan nor the rest of them, with the exception of his mother and father, knew that she was his mate. He doubted very much that it would make a difference to Khan, either.

But the fact remained, she was his other half. Standing up, he leaned over her and smelled her. He tried to tell himself that it was to see if any of her wounds were infected, but knew it for the lie that it was. He wanted her scent and nothing more. Leaving her before he did something incredibly stupid like lick her throat, he closed the door softly behind him. His mother was standing in the hall when he looked up.

"She's sleeping again. I didn't give her anything for pain because she might use that to leave—"

"Did you talk to her? Did you tell her what she is to you?"

He shook his head, frankly tired of telling her that he wasn't going to claim her.

"She'll be gone soon enough. Then what are you going to do?"

He kissed his mom's forehead and stepped back. "Nothing. I have to go into town and check on a patient. Don't wait up for me."

"What kind of patient needs you for that long? Walker Bowen, answer me this minute." He stopped on the stairs and turned to look at her. She had always been very perceptive and now was no different. "If you think going to another woman will solve your problem in that room, you're just as naïve as your brother."

"Stay out of this, Mom. This is between her and me, and I will do what I want. I'm a grown man who knows what I'm about. And have been for some time." He looked down the stairs to avoid seeing the look in her eyes. "I won't be coming back until she's able to move on her own. She's well enough in her healing that she only needs to rest and heal."

He was down the stairs and out the door before he changed his mind. His mom said his name a couple of times, but he didn't turn back. He felt like shit enough and didn't need her compounding it. It didn't help him that his brother, Dylan, was leaning against his truck when he came out.

"Wanna go for a quick run?"

Walker shook his head.

"Then how about we go into town, get roaring drunk, fuck a few girls, and hole up at my place for a few days while Khan cools off? He's pissed again."

Walker got into his truck and Dylan in the passenger side. "What about now? I swear to Christ, I'm thinking about hiring someone to get him laid so he'll relax. Maybe if he does, he'll see that we're grown men and not his children."

Both men laughed as Walker pulled out into traffic off the compound. He was about a mile out when he turned to his brother and saw that he was staring at him. Dylan, like their mom, was very good at simply waiting until someone fessed up to whatever they had done. Walker shifted on the seat and tried not to give in. But he needed to tell someone, and Dylan wouldn't tell if he asked him not to.

"She's my mate. The girl sleeping in my bed right now. She's my mate." Dylan nodded, and Walker wasn't sure if he meant he knew or to continue. Walker continued. "Her name is Caitlynne McCray. She told Dad when he asked, but to me she's.... I'm not going to claim her."

"Because of Khan."

It wasn't a question, but Walker nodded anyway.

"Thought so. You may not have claimed her, but you do smell like her a little. So how does that work? You not claiming her?"

He shrugged. "When she's better, she'll go back to wherever she came from and I'll go about my business."

"You think that'll be all it takes?"

Walker didn't know and said so.

"I don't. I'm pretty sure that once you find her, it's either claim or go fucking nut ball on her. I read somewhere that a male didn't claim his mate for whatever reason and he simply went insane until he did. Then it wasn't pretty. He was in such bad shape that he ended up raping her, and it was all she wrote after that."

Walker looked at his brother, then back at the road. "Where the hell do you get this shit? He wouldn't be able to rape her, he wouldn't be able…you're making that shit up."

"Nope. Mom has those books that she's always pushing us to read…the ones about the traits and traditions of our kind? You should read the second one…or the third, I can't remember, but it talks about all sorts of reasons for a mate to claim and what happens when you don't."

Walker didn't ask where the books were because he knew. Right now, book three was in his home, given to him by their mom a few days ago. He hadn't planned on reading it, but now thought that he should give it a try. He looked over at Dylan when he laughed.

"And trying to fuck her out of your system won't work either. I can't remember why, but I don't think you can get any satisfaction from anyone but her."

That statement nearly had him run off the road.

"Watch it, moron. I haven't found my mate yet and won't if you scar my pretty face."

"Are you seriously telling me that I won't be able to have sex with any other female but her?"

Dylan nodded, then grinned. "You can probably have sex with them, but you aren't going to get off. According to the legend, you will be able to have all the sex you want, but it will be painful because you can't get off. Also, you should know that your mate will know it too. That you go to others for your…hum, to get your rocks off. Something to do with perimeters."

"Pheromones," Walker corrected without thinking. The idea that she would know kept going through his head. How she would know was because he would be.... "What about jerking off?"

He flushed when his brother laughed. "Don't know, big brother, but I would say probably. What the hell does one know about the opposite sex anyway? Besides, I'm pretty sure that won't help you a hell of a lot either. I've not seen the girl in awhile, but I have a feeling that she's pretty and more than likely stubborn as hell. How the hell else would she have withstood what happened to her and still manage to save Dad?"

Walker had forgotten about that. To hear his dad tell it, she'd known who he was and what she was doing when she tossed the rock—or depending on the time of day he was telling it, the boulder—she'd thrown to distract the men away from them both.

He drove to the hospital and told his brother not to flirt with any of his nurses while he was gone. Walker knew Dylan was going to heed his warning like he was going to become a monk, but he did try. The patient he was seeing was an older woman who had been a friend of his mom's for nearly all her life. His mom asked him to make sure she had the best of everything. He was trying.

Mary Donald was dying. She was in her late nineties and still as sharp as the day she'd turned thirty and met his mom as a child. When his mom had shifted accidentally, Mary had kept her safe until Walker's grandparents had come to get her. She'd been an honorary pack member since.

"You said you'd be here at ten, and it's ten past. What did you find, a girl?" She looked at him hard. "You did, didn't you? Hot damn, who is the lucky mate?"

"No one. And keep your voice down. You want someone to hear your potty mouth?" He grinned at her when she snorted at him. "And I have no one in my life but you at the moment." He opened her chart and read what had been put on it last night and the day before after he'd left her. She'd had a bad night, and again last night. Walker sat on the chair and finished reading it before he looked at her. She was staring at him intently.

"Who is she? A regular girl like me?"

He nodded, knowing that if he didn't tell her, she'd hound him to death.

"And your brother, Khan, he's keeping you from her, ain't he?"

"He doesn't know about our being mates. None of them do but Dylan and Mom and Dad. And I want to keep it that way." He knew she wouldn't say anything if he asked her not to, so he wasn't really worried. "He would forbid it, and you and I both know that."

"He's been hurt bad, your brother. Can't really blame him for that. What he needs is a woman of his own to bring him around. That she-bitch, the girl he fell in love with, you know where I might find her?"

"No. And what do you plan to do if I did? Hire a hit man? I've already thought of that and it won't work. She's as human as you are, and people would begin to miss her. Especially knowing who she is."

Roseann Yates had been the woman who had hurt them all, especially Khan. She'd betrayed him so badly that it had taken nearly five years of hard work and Khan crawling so deep within himself that he had never been able to come back. And his hatred of humans, any of them, including his distrust of this woman, had been legendary. Walker looked at Mary when she touched his cheek.

"He'll come around once you tell him who she is to you. He'll have to. He won't be able to keep you two apart once you have her, and we both know that you won't be able to keep away."

"I have to. And I will." He opened the file again and started asking her what she thought they could do with her future treatments. She glared at him at first, but told him in no uncertain terms that when she died he was to simply let her.

"I've been waiting to jump off this train for some time. You have to let me go." She lifted his chin to look into his eyes. "Guess I'll have to hang around until you get this settled, but not one minute more. You bring her to see me and I'll let you know if this foolishness you're thinking about of not claiming her is gonna stick or not."

"It will." He left her twenty minutes later to find Dylan in the nurse's lounge talking to three of his staff. They weren't draped completely over him, but enough to know that had he not come in when he had, they'd all be having sex on the tiny couch in the room.

Dylan and he ended up at his house with two cases of cold beer and six large pizzas. It was near the big house on the compound, within walking distance, so Marc and Reed were going to meet them there soon. Walker worked hard at keeping his thoughts off the beautiful blue-eyed woman at his parents' house. He'd had her moved there shortly after she'd awakened the second time. He thought it best for everyone.

CHAPTER THREE

Lynne woke to the scent of food. Her belly rumbled even as she opened her eyes to see the elderly woman coming toward her. Lynne nearly fell getting up to help her with the tray, forgetting all about the wounds on her legs. The woman, who she surmised was Mrs. Bowen, fussed about good manners getting her hurt.

"Here, you eat this and it'll make you feel better." She set the bed tray over her lap after helping Lynne sit up more in the bed. Her wrist, while not broken according to the elder Mr. Bowen, was still tender from the bad sprain. "If you don't mind leaning on me a bit, I can see about getting you a spit bath."

Lynne knew what a spit bath was, but thought it a funny term, especially in this day and age. She pulled the first bit of thick broth to her mouth and nearly moaned from the taste. She was half-finished when Mrs. Bowen brought out some towels and a pail of steaming water.

"I've been trying to figure out how to wash your hair, but can't think of it. Other than carrying you in there to lean you over the tub, can't seem to come up with nary an idea to make it work. I could get George to help, but that might cause you more problems than it's going to be worth for you. Scent and all."

Lynne nodded, not having a clue what she was talking about.

"But we can get you cleaned up a little more. I did manage to get you washed up when we brought you in, but it's been a while, and I'm sure you could use a good sponging."

"I was wondering when I can leave? That other man, he said he was my doctor. He said I couldn't leave until he said so. I'm pretty sure that's considered kidnapping." Lynne thought that maybe the man was a little odd, but didn't say so to his mom. "I would like to call a cab to come and get me. I need to go to the police about those men."

Mrs. Bowen was shaking her head. "I'm afraid that you'll need to stay until he releases you. He went to a lot of trouble getting you stitched back up. But if you tell me the name of those men, we'll take care of them for you."

Lynne didn't like the way that had sounded. The woman had smiled, but it hadn't reached her eyes when she'd spoken of taking care of the Ingram's. Lynne shivered a little and finished the broth. The men who had hurt her were not mentioned again as she was helped to wash her body and change into another large t-shirt.

"There you go. I bet you're worn out now, aren't you? Walker said I could give you another shot for pain if you want."

Lynne declined.

"Well, you let me know if you change your mind."

Lynne laid there trying to breathe through the pain. She was hurting less than she had been days ago, but was still in a great deal of it. She pulled the blanket off her and looked at her leg.

She figured she could probably stand on it for all of ten seconds, but not enough to leave. She wiggled her toes, and while hurting, it wasn't sickening. She knew that if she was going to get better, she had to regain her strength. And the first thing she had to do was get her leg working again. Then there was the catheter.

She hadn't even known about it until a few minutes into her bath. She had no idea why she'd not thought of it, but now could see the reason for it. She couldn't walk. But first things first, her leg.

By the time she'd lifted it up and down off the bed ten times, she was hurting enough to call Mrs. Bowen back to give her something. She was sweating and swearing as she forced herself through ten more. Putting her leg back on the bed gently, she laid back and closed her eyes. When the door opened again, she didn't have the energy to see who it was.

"You doing all right, my dear?" She recognized Mr. Bowen's voice and nodded. "You're pale as a sheet. What have you been doing?"

"I'm going home." Sounded stupid, she knew, but he didn't say anything. She heard the chair creak and looked over at him. "Why are you here?"

"I like your company. No, that's a lie. I don't know you well enough to say that yet. I wanted some peace and quiet, and you don't seem the talkative type. My mother is visiting. She can talk the fur off a cat."

She looked at him oddly, but didn't comment.

Lynne closed her eyes when he picked up the paper and started reading it. She didn't care if he sat there. She was going to rest for a little bit, then go back at her leg. She was thinking maybe she needed to call someone when he spoke up.

"I heard that Walker was in here today. You two get anything settled?"

Other than him pissing her off and telling her she couldn't leave, they hadn't really talked all that much.

"He can be a bit stubborn, but I would imagine you can be as well."

"I would like to call someone. Do you think that would be possible?" He nodded to the phone across the room, then stood up to get it. He sat back down when she held the phone in her hand. Who she had to call was private, but could also wait. She leaned back against the headboard, wondering why she wasn't in a hospital, and why they would be safer if she wasn't.

"I wanted to ask you something. Those men that chased you, did you know them?"

She'd not told them anything, so didn't know where he'd gotten his information.

"You were talking when you were first brought here…something about someone chasing you."

She knew he was lying, and he seemed to know she knew. She didn't answer him. He didn't seem to mind too much, but continued to read the newspaper. She felt herself drifting off when the door opened and then closed again. Opening her eyes, she picked up the phone and called her boss, Conrad Garrett.

"Where the hell have you been? Do you know that I've put out a missing person's report on you?" He blustered for several more minutes before he slowed to let her answer him. She didn't really like or trust her boss, but he did seem concerned, *seemed* being the operative word. But Lynne trusted very few people, and he wasn't one of them, probably never would be.

"You told me to take some time. I'm taking it. I'm not due back for another…I don't know that right now. I've been relaxing and resting, as you bellowed at me on the seventeenth." She had no idea of the date and hoped he'd shed some light on it. "Why the hell would you call in a MP when you told me not to contact anyone until I came back?"

"Your neighbor said your window had been busted open and there was blood on your carpet. What the hell else was I supposed to think other than some ass you put away was out to get you?" That was close enough that she told him he was wrong.

"The two brothers that stole from my elderly neighbor across the street? They decided to get me for some payback. I eluded them pretty well, but not enough to avoid getting a little banged up. Can you have my window fixed? I'll pay you back."

"It's already taken care of. You want me to take care of the police report too?" She told him no, she'd do it. "All right. Let me see. You were supposed to be gone a month…no, that was six weeks. You've been on leave for nearly three, so I guess I'll talk to you in another few weeks. If you need anything, give me a call. And next time you have a beef with the neighbors, call me and let me take care of it. You can't be fucking with these people, not now at any rate."

She knew that. And she hadn't had the chance to fuck with anyone. If her calculations were right, she'd gone on R&R on the seventeenth and had been kidnapped on the first day. If she had already been gone three weeks, the date was right around the fifth of June. Shit. So much for having a long vacation to rest up on a beach as she recouped.

"I'm not at home and probably won't be for another week or so. When I get back there, I'll let you know. Any word on the Small case?" The case that had gotten her nearly killed and a vice president arrested. "And do I need to be watching over my shoulder until the trial?"

"He's still in jail. It's better than most hotels. But we have a platoon of guards surrounding him. He tries to step out, he's going to have fifty guns pointed at him." He cleared his throat before continuing. "You okay, kid? I know what it's like to lose a partner like you did."

Melvin Carpenter had been her partner for nearly six years and had taken a bullet meant for her. Had he not stood up those seconds before she had, she would have taken one in the head and not him. She looked out the window as she thought about what his brains and—

"Do me a favor, will you, and don't bring it up again right now. I'm dealing, but…I don't want to think about it until I'm facing that bastard in the courtroom."

"Okay, kid."

They talked a few more seconds before she hung up. For whatever reason, she knew he was tracking the call and didn't want him to know about the Bowens. He told her to let him know if she needed anything and she promised she would, both of them knowing that she wouldn't call him if her life depended on it. She knew that he was involved somehow, and for that reason she didn't trust him. Just as she was putting the phone on the bedside table, the door opened. The man standing there was huge, bigger than Dr. Bowen, and he seemed to be pissed about something. She reached for the gun that wasn't there and waited.

~~~

Khan didn't know what to expect, but the beauty before him wasn't it. He shut the door behind him to give himself a few seconds to compose his thoughts. This wasn't going to go well and he was preparing himself for the tears and begging, like all women like her did.
~~~

"I've come to tell you that as soon as you're able, I'd like for you to make other arrangements on where to stay." He watched her for the sudden tears. She only nodded. "Do you hear what I'm telling you? I want you out of here as soon as possible."

"I can hear just fine, and since you seem to think I'm deaf and need to yell, I can only imagine that people down the street heard you. And I'd like nothing better than to oblige you. If you think you can take this piss bag off me, I might be able to move around enough to get some exercise."

He flushed, forgetting that she had been bedridden since she'd been brought in.

"I don't have a clue how to remove it. Perhaps you can ask my brother. He's the doctor." She snorted. He wasn't sure what to say to her now. "Do you need anything? I'm not going to give you money, but I can accommodate you in other ways."

"I didn't ask to be brought here or for your money, jerk ass. I have plenty of my own and, as for accommodating me, fuck off. I want out of here as badly as you want me to be." He was lost. He had expected her to want to stay, and now he didn't know what to say back to her. "You find that ass of a brother of yours, have him remove this thing, and I'll be more than happy to go to my house. Today, if it can be arranged."

Khan turned his back to her and opened the door. He could see his mother coming up the stairs toward them when he turned back to the girl. He glared at her. "You'd better be nice to my mother or, so help me, you won't be able to hide deep enough where I won't—"

She cut him off, her voice low and threatening. "You mother-fucking asshole. You think you can come in here and treat me like some piece of shit, then threaten me with being nice to your mother? Fuck you and the horse you rode in on."

She sat up in the bed, and he noticed that she was pale and her shoulder was bleeding. "Get the fuck out of here. And don't bother coming back. If I have to, I will rip this fucker out to get up and tear you a new ass. Get out."

He moved out of the way, letting his mom move past him. She had to have heard them arguing, but she only smiled at the girl as she put the tray over her lap. She turned back to him and crossed her arms over her chest. "You heard her. She would very much like it if you left. I'm thinking it might be best if you did." He nodded, but before he could make good his escape, she spoke again. "Khan Bowen, don't think you're off the hook. You and I will be having a conversation about threats to a guest in my house. Do you understand me?"

"Yes, ma'am. I understand." He looked back at her and dropped his head. "I'm sorry for being rude to someone in your home."

"And?"

He looked up and knew what she wanted, but she wasn't going to get it. Nor was the girl. He would not apologize to a human, especially a female one.

He left the room without another word. His mom would be pissed, more than a little too, but he wasn't going to bow down to anyone like the human again. And he was not impressed with her. He was appalled at her behavior, not impressed at all.

He was out the door when he remembered his dad. He'd asked to speak to him before he left, but Khan wasn't in the mood now. He tore off his shirt and shifted even as his pants were settling on the ground.

Roseann had been like the girl in the bedroom upstairs. Conniving and vicious, she had made him fall in love with her. Then she'd not only betrayed him, but his family as well. He would never trust another human as long as he lived.

Khan had known she wasn't his mate…hell, they all had, but she was everything he had wanted in one, except for being a panther. And when he'd told her what he was, even going so far as to show her, she'd seemed just fine about it. But he'd been wrong, nearly dead wrong.

She'd had him over one night and told him she was having a few friends over as well. He'd asked her to marry him the week before and she'd said yes. The big wedding had been planned for June…June nearly seven years ago.

He shuddered when he thought of the events that had followed and cringed when he thought of how he'd handled it. Her family, wealthy and prestigious, had made it difficult for him to return to a normal life and even more difficult to return to the job he'd loved so much.

Khan stopped when he saw Dylan at Walker's house. He'd been going there to talk his brother into releasing the girl to where she belonged. When they went into Walker's house, Khan nearly went back to his own home, but decided to get this over with. The girl needed to be gone.

There were things for each of them at all their houses, including his. There were places that hid each of their clothes in the forest beyond, as well. Khan went there now. He pulled on his jeans and was unfolding his shirt when he knocked on the door. Walker didn't look surprised to see him and invited him in.

"We're having pizza and beer. If you can remain civil, you can stay. Otherwise, you can leave now."

Khan wanted to snap that he was always civil, but remembered how uncivilized he had been to the girl.

"I mean it, Khan. I'm not in the mood for your shit tonight."

He nodded and walked in. Whatever had happened to his brother must have been bad. Walker was usually the least tempered of them all. Khan was in the kitchen when his cell phone went off. He turned it off when he saw who it was. He would take his punishment later from his mom. Right now, he wanted to speak to his brother.

"When will that girl be gone?" He'd managed to make it until the pizza was delivered before saying what he'd really come there for. Walker didn't answer at first, but Dylan had plenty to say.

"What do you care? She's not hurting you, and she certainly isn't sponging off you, either. And as far as I could see the other day, Mom and Dad seem to like her." Dylan snorted. "'Course, they don't hate every person they come in contact with like you do."

He wanted to hit him, but was in enough trouble with doing things in other people's houses already. He looked over at Walker, ignoring Dylan. He decided to ignore him and get to the problem at hand.

"She'll leave when I say so. You can fuck off for all I care." Dylan started to say something, but Walker stopped him with a look. "You don't like that, then you can leave now. I'm not releasing her until she's healthy."

"What's going on?" He looked at Dylan, then at Walker. "You know something about this girl that you don't want me to know. She's a fucking reporter, isn't she? Mother fuck, Walker, do we want to go through that again?"

"As a matter of fact, I don't know what she does for a living. She didn't even tell me her name. So Dad told me." Khan noticed that he didn't answer him about what he knew. Before he could ask again, Dylan spoke.

"You might not be able to tell him, but I fucking don't have a problem with it. She's his mate."

Khan staggered back and looked at both men. Walker was saying something to Dylan, but Khan couldn't understand. His entire world had just narrowed down to a pinpoint.

CHAPTER FOUR

By the next morning, she was so sore she could barely hold her arms up without screaming. Her leg was pounding in pain, but she wasn't going to stop. No pain, no gain was what she kept telling herself when she tried to lift her leg again. But as soon as it was off the bed, she did cry out. Then the door crashed open to the room.

"What the hell is going on?" Dr. Bowen was standing before her in a pair of boxers and the most beautiful body she'd ever seen. "Who is attacking you?"

"Get out." She hated the way her voice sounded breathless, and she pointed to the door again. "I told you yesterday I didn't want to see you again…what the fuck are you doing?"

He'd taken the covers from her and tossed them off. She glanced down at the blood-soaked bandages and tried to get the blanket back over it when he tore them from her fingers and threw them on the floor.

"What have you been doing? You've opened the wounds again. Now I'm going to have to see what you've done."

She tried not to stare at his body, but Christ, he was not giving her much choice. Even as pain riddled as she was, he was making her wish he would take off the rest of his clothes and join her in the big bed. He stopped suddenly and looked at her.

He appeared...well, hungry came to mind, and she reached for the pillow next to her and covered herself with it. He didn't move, and neither did she for several seconds. When he came toward her, she fully expected him to hit her and braced herself for the blow.

"Do you know what you do to me when you smell like that?" He was standing over her and she could see his cock harden beneath the shorts. "Caitlynne, if you don't want me to join you in that bed, pain or no pain, you had better say something."

She thought of a thousand ways to say "yes," but only shook her head. He took a step back, then another before he took a deep breath. He didn't look any happier that far away than he had close up. And his cock seemed to agree with him about getting into bed with her.

"I want to leave. Today. Now." He didn't move, so she tried again. "I want to go home, and I want...no, I demand that you take this thing out of me so I can go."

"And what do you think will happen when you do leave? Do you think someone is going to help you around? How will you feed yourself? How will you move without help?"

She glared at him. "I've been shot before, and I know how to take care of myself. I don't need anyone to cater to my every whim."

He looked shocked. She wasn't sure if it was her tone or the fact that she'd been shot before. He stepped toward her again and didn't stop until he was almost on top of her.

"Who are you?"

She looked away, somehow knowing that he would know if she was lying.

"What is it you do that got you into the mess we found you in?"

The need to answer was nearly overwhelming. She looked back at him and frowned. "Nothing. When you found me, it was because I was being a good Samaritan. I doubt I'll go that route ever again."

Walker dropped to his knees, and when she tried to look away, he pulled her chin back to face him. He looked at her with such intensity that she felt his gaze all over her body. When his eyes seemed to center on her mouth, she licked her lips. His moan made her feel things she'd never felt before.

"I want to kiss you, Caitlynne." Without thought to what that would mean for either of them, she leaned toward him. "Caitlynne."

First contact was a brush of his lips. The second, more. His hand moved to the back of her head, and he took her lower lip into his mouth and suckled. She moaned this time; her entire being needed more from him. But he pulled back and she could only stare at him.

"As much as I'd like to take this to the very end, I'm afraid that you're not up for it." He kissed her again, this time longer; his tongue danced with hers. Then he lifted his head. "Christ, I would like nothing more than to bury myself deep in—"

The door opened and there stood Khan. She didn't know why he'd been coming in, but he was on top of Walker in seconds. The two of them were going to kill each other if they weren't stopped. One of them, or both, could get seriously hurt. She reached for the closest thing she could touch and held it in her hand, waiting for the moment she could use it.

The pitcher of water flew across the room. Her intent was to hit them both, but she only managed to hit Khan. And when it broke on his forehead, he fell back on the floor with a thud. She looked around for another weapon when Walker turned toward her. He was breathing hard and looked…well, she didn't know what exactly was different about him, but he was bigger, it seemed.

"You all right?"

She nodded at his question.

"Good. Don't move from that spot. I need to get help with him and I don't want you to get cut."

His voice was calm. She didn't know how to react to it so she nodded again. She glanced at Khan when Walker stepped out of the room. Then she swung her legs off the side of the bed and tried to stand. She was getting her ass out of there. These people were certifiable.

The first step on her injured leg nearly took her breath away. She almost fell over the catheter tubing and had to count to ten when she came down oddly on her leg. Once she was moving toward what she hoped was the bathroom, things didn't get much better.

Sweat poured off her, but she knew she'd have to get over it. But before she could get to the bathroom, she was scooped up into someone's arms. She tried to fight back.

"Don't hurt yourself. It's me." She glared at Walker, who was laughing. "You're a hellcat, aren't you? I thought I said to stay put."

"I'm not a dog to mindlessly obey chauvinistic men like you. Put me down." He did, but back on the bed. "I'm leaving before he wakes up. He's not going to be happy with me when he does. And I'm reasonably sure he hated me in the first place."

His entire demeanor changed. "What did he say to you? So help me, if he hurt you in any way, I will rip his throat out."

"She looks like she could hold her own with him." George walked in and smiled at her. "Pissed you off, did he? Good for you. Come on, Walker. Let's get him to safer grounds so you can pick the glass out."

"She thinks she's leaving. I can't...she can't leave just yet. She's not fully he—"

"She's sitting right here, you moronic asshole. And if you have something to say about me or something you assume that I will do, I would prefer that you said it to me and not around me."

George laughed and didn't seem fazed when Walker glared at him. "Oh, she'll do just fine. Just fine indeed." George laughed again as he continued. "I'll sit with her for a spell. Your mother is getting the kitchen ready for your surgery."

Lynne watched two more men come in and pick Khan up as if he didn't weigh a ton. The other two, more than likely brothers to Khan and Walker because of their matching looks, seemed to find it funny that she had knocked the man on his ass. She looked over at George. "Is he going to be all right?"

George nodded.

"He attacked without provocation. He's lucky that I didn't...."

"Didn't what?"

She looked away. She'd nearly said lucky she didn't shoot him.

"Lynne, you've never told us who those men were that hurt you. We can't help you if you don't let—"

"He kissed me." She didn't know why she blurted that out, but once she did it seemed to open a dam. "I don't know why, but he made me feel things. Why would he kiss me, and why would Khan come in and attack like that?"

"He was hurt. Khan was hurt by a…by someone much like you. He is bitter and cold, and I despair of him ever getting over her." He looked through the open door when there was cursing from beyond it. "He needs someone to love him so that he'll trust again."

Lynne was still trying to wrap her mind around the fact that he said someone like her. What did this man know or think he knew? She had to get out of there. And short of taking the catheter with her on her own, she was coming up short on plans.

~~~

Walker would have taken the glass out without numbing his brother's head, but his mother was standing right there. She was eyeing him as if she knew what he had been planning. She more than likely did. Walker stretched his neck muscles again and tried to steady his hands.

"You're trying to slow this down on purpose just so I can't get up. Well, it won't work. She's leaving right now."

His mom hit Khan in the back of the head hard and then glared at him when he looked ready to stand up. "You'll sit right there or so help me, Khan Bowen, I will take you to the wood shed." She hit him again in the shoulder. "What were you thinking attacking your brother like that? Were you hoping to scare that poor woman so much she'd run?"

"She doesn't belong here. And he told me that he wasn't going to claim her. And what did I see when I walked into that bedroom? He was all over her. Practically throwing her back on the bed and mating with her."

Walker growled and pulled a large piece of glass from Khan's head without trying to be gentle. He threw down his instruments and stepped away from Khan before he murdered him. "I'm releasing her today." Walker left them standing there to go to the bedroom where Lynne was. She was sitting
~~~

in the bed, looking out the window, and his dad was going a mile a minute.

"Hello, son. Get Khan straightened out?"

He nodded at his dad as he pulled out his cell and dialed. "Hello, Jane, this is Doctor Bowen. Could you please make arrangements to come to my parents' home? I have a patient that needs to be dismissed." He didn't look at Caitlynne or his dad as she made arrangements to come right over. "She'll need a ride back to her home. Can you give her a lift?"

After everything was settled, he turned to the two of them. His father looked sad, but Caitlynne looked…he was thinking she looked like she had nothing on her mind, but that wasn't right, either. She looked indifferent, maybe even bored. He started to speak when his dad stood up.

"Well, I guess…I guess it was nice meeting you, Lynne. I'm sorry that you couldn't recuperate here, but things…." He looked at Walker, then at Caitlynne again. "Things aren't always what you hope for."

His dad walked out of the room with a pat on his back. Walker looked back at Caitlynne and she turned away from him. He wasn't sure what to say to her so he simply leaned against the dresser and waited for Jane. She would be there very soon as she was a group member and lived not far from his parents. The doorbell chimed four minutes later, and he heard his nurse on the steps. Walker stepped into the hall to talk to her.

"I need you to remove her catheter and help her to dress. She's no doubt going to need something for pain when you get her home. I'll give you something to take with you so you can give it to her." He tried to tell himself he was doing the right thing. "Don't tell anyone where you take her, Jane. She's been hurt because someone was chasing her." Not entirely true, but she had been hurt, and probably by him and

Khan more than she'd been hurt physically by those men. He glanced at the closed door again before continuing. "If she starts to bleed again or needs…anything, I want you to take her to…take her to…." He didn't know where to have her taken.

But Jane patted his arm. "I don't know what's going on here, but I'll take care of her for you. You just leave it to me, Doc. I've got her for you."

Walker nodded and started down the hallway. He was being a coward, and more than that, he was being an ass. He wanted more than anything to go back up there and kiss her again. Tell her things were going to be fine, that he and Khan would work this out, but he was reasonably sure that they never would, and he'd be lying to the one woman in the world he was supposed to love above everything else. Walker left the house without stopping to speak to anyone. He was glad now he'd pulled on his pants before going for his brother's throat when Caitlynne had hit Khan. He walked to his car he'd left there the night before when he'd brought Reed home and drove to his house.

His mate. His mate was within ten miles of him and he was alone in his house. When his phone rang, he knew who it was immediately by the ringtone and ignored it. He wasn't in the mood to speak to anyone, especially not his mom and dad.

There were times when he didn't much care for his brother, Khan. Khan had been wrong to tell him he forbade him to see Caitlynne. Khan had been equally wrong to have attacked him, especially in front of Caitlynne. Moving to the kitchen, Walker tried to remember the last time his brother had been out…or for that matter, the last time he'd laughed.

Walker pulled a beer out of the refrigerator and stood in the kitchen, drinking it. He wasn't the least bit surprised to see his brother knocking at the door a few minutes later.

Walker let Marc in and told him to get himself something to drink.

"Her name is Caitlynne April McCray, and she lives at—" Marc began.

"I don't want to know."

He sat at the table while Marc continued with a nod. "She lives in a house. What she does for a living might surprise you. It certainly did me. I just don't—"

Walker cleared his throat, knowing that once Marc started, he'd never stop.

"Right. She's a schoolteacher. Junior high home economics, as a matter of fact."

"Schoolteacher? Which do you not believe? The teacher part or the home economics part?" He tried to imagine her standing in front of a room full of adolescent boys and couldn't do it. She was more of a…. "Are you sure she's not like the shop teacher or something?"

Marc laughed. "Nah. Home economics, like I said."

Walker waited for him to continue and decided that he was going to kill more than one of his siblings today. When nothing more was forthcoming, he realized that Marc wasn't in the room. Physically he was, but his mind had wandered. He waited, knowing that he'd come back sooner or later.

"There's too much money in her account. Not to mention she has really nice digs, too. Something out of one of those house fashion mags Mom is always buying."

Red flags were going off everywhere in Walker's mind, and he wasn't even an investigator like Marc was.

"Could be she just does a really awesome job, but her bi-monthly deposits make me think she works for someone higher on the food chain."

"You think she's into selling drugs? Or something along those lines?"

Marc shook his head.

"What then?"

"Her house and truck are locked up tight. But there's something…off about them. The truck is too low to the ground, and her house? I'm thinking that whoever broke her window a week ago had to have been better than those idiots that had her. The kind of people I'm talking about play for keeps. The security system she has in place is expensive and very smart. She knew what she was having put in and why. I just wish I knew her well enough to ask her if I could look at it closer. Am I going to get to know her better, Walker?"

He didn't answer him.

He and Marc had steaks on the grill and two baked potatoes each. Neither of them was into girly salads, and he didn't even bother with mushrooms or anything else to take away from his rare sixteen-ounce steaks. Marc didn't seem to mind, either.

They talked about nothing at all, and when they were out on his deck at sunset, Marc brought up Caitlynne again. He was like a dog with a fat bone.

"You had me investigate, yet you let her go back to her home. There are any number of reasons I can think of as to why you'd do that, but I know the real one."

Walker didn't bother answering.

"She's either your mate or she owes you money. I dismissed the second one right away because she has more than you, even on pay day. So she's gotta be your mate."

"You got it," Walker confirmed.

Marc didn't gloat, nor did he ask again why he had sent her away. So he told him. "Khan told me…no, that's not right, he forbade me to see her."

"No fuck? Sheesh, I wish he'd get laid or something. Can he even do that?"

Walker shook his head.

"Not the getting laid part. I'm pretty sure no woman would come near him without him snarling at her. But you're going to mate with her anyway, right? Or are you going to let him rule you?"

"Yes. For now." Walker looked out over the woods behind his house. "She and I kissed today, and when Khan came in and started to show me how much larger he is than me, she…she knocked him on his ass with a water pitcher. I pulled out the glass and let him deal with it afterwards. I sent her home so she and I couldn't get any closer."

Marc snorted. "You think that's going to work, you sending her away? I don't. You're an idiot if you think that."

So did Walker. He wondered how long he'd last before he tried to find her.

CHAPTER FIVE

The crutches weren't doing her a bit of good. They had the first day and then into the second, but now she had tossed them across the room and glared at them every time she tried to make her body cooperate with what she was doing.

When Jane had brought her home three days ago, Lynne tried to remember why she was in an all-fired hurry to leave. Then she'd think of that jackass Khan and would get pissed all over again. Lynne wondered what his problem was as she made her way to the kitchen. She nearly tripped over the rug when someone knocked on her back door.

Jane. The woman had been coming over on her way to work every day. She was entirely too chipper for her tastes, but she did seem to love her job of taking care of people. She opened the door, but blocked her entrance.

"You should be using your crutches, not walking around yet."

Lynne nodded, but didn't move.

"If you let me in, I'll share the pizza I have."

Pizza. Caitlynne loved pizza, and when Jane showed her the box, it was all she could do not to knock her down and take it from her. It was from her favorite place. And from the scents coming from the box, it was one that was covered in meat and cheese and everything else they had in the kitchen.

"The guy who owns the place knows you." Jane got down some paper plates when Lynne showed her where they were. "I noticed the pizza boxes in the fridge and figured you've been there. When I mentioned your name, he knew just what kind you liked. He said to call him sometime and he'll give you the news."

Lynne nearly bobbled the glass of wine. She set it down and sat with Jane as she took out the first slice. She'd have to get rid of her sooner rather than later now. She would have to call Omar and find out what he knew.

"I've been ordering from him since I moved here. They have the best pizza." They did too. Omar Sanders was one of her workers, one of her snitches. "I order one at least once or twice a week."

"Yeah, that's what he said. Said you hadn't been around lately. I told him you'd been injured a week or so back. He said he knew." She frowned as she took another slice. "How do you suppose he knew that?"

Because she'd been injured two weeks ago on information that he had given her. It wasn't his fault that the information was only half there, and she'd already told him she was fine. But because of her injuries, it was the reason that she'd been sleeping so soundly the night the idiots had broken in. She'd taken a pain pill so she could sleep after talking with her boss for over an hour beforehand.

Lynne shrugged. "He's the best, but a little off his rocker. That was awesome pizza. How much do I owe you for saving me from having to cook for myself?"

"Nothing. It was fun and I like talking to you." Jane looked at her watch as she stood up. "I need to get going.

Working a double tonight. Thanks, Lynne. It was really nice for me too. I hate to cook."

"Me too." Jane went out the door and Lynne was just shutting it when she caught something out the corner of her eye. Waving at Jane and making a production of slipping around on the wet decking, she saw who was there.

"Mother fuck," she said low and to herself as Jane drove away. She made her limp more pronounced as she made her way into the house, pulling out her cell as she went. "Agent McCray to speak to leader Garrett." She recited the numbers that were given to her when she was first trained. "I have a code seven twenty-three."

"Stand by, Agent McCray, while I find him." The girl's tone was nervous and full of terror. Lynne knew that had she shown up rather than called, the girl would have pissed herself. Lynne wasn't your everyday agent.

"Where?"

Lynne told him the precise location of the man across the street when he came on the line.

"I'm sending a sleeper to you. For Christ's sake, don't fucking shoot this one."

One time. One time she shot the guy sent to protect her and it's like she did it every day. She went to the front room, pulled up the sight to locate the camera she had mounted on her roof, and turned it toward the man standing there.

"Gray sweat pants, green and navy sweatshirt. He has on tennis shoes, running and high top. He has on a cap and his…you might want to tell the sleeper he's armed. I think it's a Glock, but can't be sure since he has it in his hand." She heard him tell someone to be careful, and she smiled. She thought maybe she'd taught him a few of those words. He came back on the line.

"You have that good of a view of him, why the hell didn't you tell me in the first place?"

She hadn't told Garrett about her extras she'd put on her house a few months ago.

"I don't suppose you know if he has on clean underwear, do you?"

She might not be able to see if they were clean, but she could see that they were white. She zoomed in on who she thought was the sleeper as he walked toward him. She had never understood why Garrett had called them sleepers. He had told her once it was because they could go past you as if in a dream. Bullshit. She knew every time one was near her.

"He has him in his sights. He said that he doesn't see a gun."

Lynne snorted when she herself could see he was armed, and knew that Garrett was lying to her again.

"He's about five yards away."

By the time the sleeper was about ten feet away, the man had seen him. He turned in the opposite direction and started walking away. Lynne was no longer watching the sleeper, but the man who had staked out her house. When he slipped around the corner and out of her sight she waited. This was, she was sure, far from over. The car coming around the same corner had her watching in fascination as the sleeper was gunned down.

"He said he's got a make on the man. The sleeper said for you to slip out the back and to a safe house."

Lynne made no comment as she watched the car drive by her house fast. She got a great picture of the man driving as he looked right at the camera for her. "Which safe house?" She rewound the recording and froze it on the face. She blew it up until she could make out features without distorting the image.

"The sleeper is coming back in now."

Lynne didn't move.

"He said to tell you that the area is clear, that it should be safe for you to move to the safe house now."

If Lynne didn't know before that Garrett was bad news, she did now. He was lying and wanted her out in the open. She looked out the back door to her house and thought about what he had said. Out the back. He wanted her to go out the back. He had another operative out there, or someone that he had sold her to.

Lynne printed the picture and downloaded all the information she had on the computer until now. She needed to make a quick escape before they got trigger-happy. She reached for her backpack as she spoke to Garrett. "I'm on crutches. I took a tumble when I was going upstairs. I don't suppose you can have him wait a damned minute." Her mind was whirling as to how to proceed as she put her Bluetooth in her ear to move while talking to him. "Let me get dressed, then I'll meet him in the alley behind my house. Can he do that?"

"Sure. Let me get in touch with him." As he spoke to someone else again, she hobbled up the stairs and gathered all her identifications she had stashed and her guns. She might be going out into the unknown, but she wasn't going to go down without a fight. The sudden knock at her door startled her.

Going down the stairs slowly, she looked in the peep hole and nearly laughed. She doubted that Walker would understand her insanity right now, so she tried to straighten up her face and opened the door. He looked good enough to eat.

"I was just—"

She cut him off with her mouth. She didn't want whoever was watching the house to know who he was. But her plan took a nice turn until she heard the phone bark in her ear.

"Lynne, how much longer are you going to be? Damn it, girl, you need to get your ass in gear."

She took a reluctant step back and put her finger to her mouth when Walker started to speak.

"Lynne?"

"I'm here. Christ, will you give me a break? I have to get dressed and then I need to make sure I'm not being followed." She handed her truck keys to Walker. "And I have to make sure that I can come back here to a house that's not been stripped empty."

She found a piece of paper and wrote Walker a note. *"Go to garage. Don't start truck until you disengage the safety mech. It's under the steering wheel just under the ticker. Turn it to the left."*

He looked at her oddly, but turned to go. Before he was out the door he turned back, pulled her to his body, and kissed her again. When he moved out this time, she stood there for several seconds, trying to get her heart to slow to a reasonable speed again.

She grabbed up the rest of her things and handed them to Walker when he came back inside. She looked around, trying to think if there was anything in the house she couldn't replace or live without. Nothing. She went to the wall nearest the stove and flipped down the little door. Pressing in the code, she nodded to the garage again. Walker took the last of her things and frowned at the gun in her hand. She would have to explain a few things to him, but right now she didn't have time.

"Hey, Garrett. Do you suppose you could send in the guy? I'm having problems getting my crutches under me and my overnight bag." He said he would. "Tell him to knock on the back door three times and I'll come let him in."

"He'll be there in about five seconds."

She looked at the timer on the computer pad. Close, but not too bad.

When they were in the truck, she turned to Walker. "Don't move until I tell you to. Once the house blows, you'll need to drive straight out the back. This part of the garage is safe."

"And you'll tell me what the hell is going on?"

She nodded even though it sounded more like a demand than a question.

"I want to know what the hell I just—"

The house blew. She didn't know where he had parked, but if he parked in her driveway, then his vehicle was toast, too, or soon would be. As soon as she told him to go, he gunned it out the now missing wall in what was once the back. He moved along the debris-covered yard like the hounds of hell were after him.

"My truck is on fire."

She glanced back and saw it was. Using the small remote on her phone, she punched in another code, and his truck exploded in flames as it reached for the sky. As it came back down to rest on the large hole that was once her yard, it exploded again, this time obliterating the entire thing.

~~~

Walker didn't say anything. Actually, he wasn't sure what to say, or even to ask. She'd blown up his truck as well as her house. He glanced over at her and could see that she was in pain, and a great deal of it. He wanted to let her suffer, but couldn't. Reaching into his pocket, he pulled out the prescription that he had picked up for her when Jane had said
~~~

her pain pills had been lost. He wondered, not for the first time, if she'd lost them on purpose.

She stared at it for several seconds before she popped it in her mouth and swallowed it dry. He knew then she was hurting more than he could see. He turned where she said and decided that he'd been patient enough. "What is it you do for a living?" He thought that was the best way to start. "I know you claim to be a school teacher, but I think that's bullshit now."

"I work for the United States government. I also work with the CIA when they need me. The house was mine and I will pay you for the truck." He didn't think it could get more surreal than it was right now. "My boss, an operative for a group of people that the CIA doesn't control, just tried to have me killed. As I think on it, he is probably the reason those other men were able to get into my house so easily. He helped them."

"The men who were chasing you."

She nodded.

"And now that you have no house, where do we go?"

"*I* go to my own version of a safe house after I drop you off somewhere." She laid her head back and closed her eyes. "There's a hotel up Route Forty that you can stay at until I make arrangements for you to get another vehicle."

As she listed to the side, he wondered if she thought he was actually going to leave her after this. When her head leaned onto his shoulder, he shifted on the seat and helped her lay across his lap. He didn't know what the hell was going on, but he was reasonably sure that whatever it was she wasn't going to tell him willingly. He decided that he was going to keep her safe even if she shot him.

Smiling, Walker pulled out his cell phone and called his brother. Khan answered on the first ring. This was not going to go well from his tone. At this point Walker was pretty sure he didn't care.

"I'm with Caitlynne. And I won't be coming back there until you can be civil to her and treat her as my mate."

When Khan cursed, Walker simply hung up. He was ready to toss the phone out the window when it rang again. He answered because the caller ID said his dad.

"You pissed him off something horrible. You tell him to fuck off or else?"

Walker laughed at his dad's humor.

"I hope to hell so. Someone needs to put him in a place where he needs to see reason."

"I won't be coming home again until he can promise me he'll treat her respectfully." His dad laughed again. "Do you think that's even possible?"

"Yes. And as much as I hate to agree with you, I think this is best. Keep me in the loop, son. I don't want anything to happen to…. That girl, didn't Jane say she lived on Blueberry Avenue?"

"Yes. And yes, it was her house. I'll explain to you later." As soon as he figured it out. "I'm going to stay with her. I don't know where yet, but I'll be in touch."

He ended up at a hotel on the same route she'd said, but not sure which one she had thought of, Walker had chosen this one because it had doors on the ground level and he could see the highway. He had watched enough spy movies to know that a person wanted to be able to get back out on the road at a moment's notice.

Walker had told the man that it was he and his wife taking up residency in their place. He had no idea what she would think about that, but right now, he didn't care. After he put her on the bed and brought in the bags she had handed him, he sat down in the room's only chair and looked at her.

She was beautiful. He had noticed that before, but now that she was resting and healthy he saw that her skin was a creamy white with a small amount of freckles spread across her nose and cheeks. He loved her long hair, red as a blazing sun, and she had the most amazing colored eyes. He thought he'd never think of them as simply blue again. He then looked over at the bags.

He was reasonably sure that one of them held guns. He skipped over it to look at the other two. One had been in the truck already and he discovered it had clothes in it. He'd looked before bringing it in because he wasn't sure if he should or not.

The next one held what he thought was a laptop. It had the shape and weight of one of the midsized ones, but he wasn't sure. He didn't want to snoop, but he did want to know. The last bag was about medium-sized, and though not heavy, he was sure it held things he didn't want to know about. He looked back at the one that held most of his attention.

"They're guns and ammo."

He looked over at her and flushed. He didn't want her to think he was some ass who'd gone through her things.

"You can open it if you want, but after you do I'm going to leave here. I have to get as much distance between you and me as I can. He might have someone looking for me."

"No." He got up and stretched, and watched her eyes darken. "You aren't going anywhere without me."

She swallowed twice and his cock leapt. She might not be as immune to him as he had thought after the fight with Khan. He moved toward the bed as he took off his shirt. "I'm tired and a little on edge. I'm going to lie down beside you and you'll keep your hands off me." He grinned when she sputtered. "Then, when we wake up, we'll discuss this relationship. Oh, and by the way, I have the truck keys, so unless you want to leave on foot, and I'm betting you won't get far, I suggest that you stay put."

"You can't talk to me like that, and we do not have anything to discuss, so you'll give me my keys and—" He took off his shirt and sat on the edge of the bed. "You can't do this. Sleep on the chair."

"I'm not sleeping in that chair. Move over and be quiet." He lay down and pulled the covers over them both. Throwing his arm over his eyes, he waited for her to try and leave or to settle down. When she lay down as far away as she could, he chuckled. She was not going to be one of those stay at home and hearth kind of mates, but more the kick his ass for not taking out the trash kind. He was going to love every minute of it.

"This isn't funny. Those bastards play for keeps, and they will kill whoever they can and do whatever it is to get what they want."

He was too tired to try to reason that out and told her so.

"It means, jackass, that when they find me, if they find me, and you're with me, you'll be as dead as me."

He pulled her into his arms and held her to him. "Then we'd better not let that happen. Go to sleep, Caitlynne. I'm seriously tired."

CHAPTER SIX

Conrad watched the video three more times, trying to figure out what had happened. He'd been watching the house for several months and knew that he had the right one. She'd been going in and out of the shit hole the entire time. What he didn't know was how her body hadn't turned up in the explosion.

"They found that sleeper you used. His body was blown nearly thirty feet from the explosion site. The cops said if the neighbor hadn't found him in their pool they might not have known he was there."

Conrad looked up at his trusted aide as he continued.

"They are also saying that it was a major gas leak and it might be months before they can sort through it all to find out. But there was no one in the house when it went up."

Because she had escaped somehow. He looked again at the house as it had gone up before the feed had fuzzed out. The blast had taken out his camera, so he had no idea what had happened in the seconds after. Except, of course, that her truck that had been parked in the driveway had blown up seconds after the first blast.

"Any of the neighbors see anything?"

Nestor Carvey shook his head.

"How the hell is that possible in a neighborhood that small?"

"There were no houses on either side of her. The house across the street has an older woman in it that had no idea there had been an explosion until I knocked on her door. She had to have been all of 300 years old and probably as deaf as a post. The other two houses—the owners were at work and only came home when it hit the news. And they said they didn't have much contact with her other than seeing her in the yard leaving or coming. And, of course, there were the idiots that we hired to kidnap her and bring her to us. They won't be talking to anyone ever again."

Conrad nodded. The Ingrams had come up with their own plans concerning McCray and he hadn't been happy about it. Not only had he ordered them killed, but had made it so no one would find their bodies for some time. Then this happened. Now the cops were bound to go to the house and find what had been done to them when they'd stashed them in the basement wrapped up in tarps. Christ, this was a major fuck up.

He pulled up the video again. He was missing something. Conrad wondered again who had decided to put the camera on rotate so he only got a view of the house when the camera swung around again. He waited for the feed to come around as he watched her truck pull into the drive, then back again when the house was there with the truck in the driveway. The third time around, it showed the house go. He looked at the truck from the first two times the camera rolled by it and tried to see if she had anyone in it with her when Nestor spoke.

"I looked into the fall she said she had. There are no records of her going to the hospital or even the company doctor. I'm thinking she was either lying, which we both know she's a pro at, or she simply took care of herself."

"She wouldn't go to the company man. She never liked him in the first place." Conrad laughed. "With good reason, I suppose. He's one of mine."

When he brought up the video this time, he paused it on the truck. He kept staring at it when Nestor spoke again.

"The police are looking for her landlord. They can't seem to reach him. And I've put in a search for him on my own. He lives in England with his fifth wife, and they have another home in France. As soon as I get a number for him there, I'll try."

Conrad didn't think he'd find one, but stared at the truck. "What kind of vehicle does she drive? I know it's a truck, but what can you tell me about it?"

"Dark blue with tinted windows. It doesn't have a cab on the back. She said she hated them. And she—"

Conrad stood up. "It's not hers. The truck, it's someone else's. This one in the camera, it's dark green and has a tool box in the back. Mother fuck, she took off in that monster she drives. Tell me what you know about it."

Nestor was shaking his head, and Conrad wanted to scream at him. "Nothing, sir. She bought it as a personal and never turned in the paperwork on it. She's only had it for about a month, but even in all that time she never registered it, nor has she ever driven it to work. The only reason I know what I do about it is because I had told her I had gotten my new tool box put in mine and she told me about disliking them. The color came up because she said hers was dark blue and not the piss green mine is. I don't believe that it's even remotely that color."

Conrad had to agree with McCray. It was the ugliest shade of green he'd ever seen. And he didn't believe for one minute that her truck was blue any longer. It was more than likely the dark green one he was looking at. After turning off the computer, he walked to his couch and sat down with a huff. Nestor sat across from him with the scowl that was forever a part of his uniform.

"I want you to see what you can find in satellite and tell me if there are any other vehicles in the area. All of them. Also, get me Intel and have them look into her new truck. If she's had it as long as you say, then she's driven it somewhere and it would have to be registered." Nestor scribbled while Conrad thought.

He wanted her dead before the trial. He knew that she was the star witness and that she had some major thing to give testimony about on Vice President Jerry Small. He also had an idea that after this, she had shit on him as well. But the vice president was the one he reported to, even though the man had been in a special jail for the past six weeks.

He'd been caught with his pants down. Literally. And not only that, but with a few too many others in the room with him. All male and all but one of them minors. But that wasn't what had gotten him in so much shit. It was the fact that he had some top secret paperwork out on his desk that one of the men had been reading over while getting a blowjob by one of the kids. Fucking idiot had been recorded and McCray had gotten it. And now they might know about all the arms deals that he and Jerry had been working on for years.

"Mr. President is on line one."

Conrad looked up at Nestor when he repeated himself.

"He wants to know what we've been able to find out about McCray. He said he expected an update over an hour ago."

The fucking president loved her, and Conrad couldn't touch her without going through hoops and circles to get her.

He took the phone from Nestor and nodded for him to leave his office.

"You were to call me an hour ago with news. Have they found her yet?"

Conrad told him no.

"She's laying low. I don't know what happened with her, but I want you to find her and make sure she's safe. I don't care what it costs the government either. Bring her home."

"Yes, sir. I'm using all my resources to do just that. I have a team in the area right now seeing—"

"You go."

Conrad nearly said for him to fuck off when Warren Russo, the president, continued.

"I want you to go there and make them see that she is a treasure to this country. We have to find her. I will have a team standing by to go to her aid if she even has a nail broken."

The fucking prick was making his life a living hell and Conrad wanted nothing more than to go to the White House and shoot the motherfucker in the head. But he took a deep breath and tried for calmness. "She might not even be there if she managed to escape the explosion. Or she might be buried under all that rubble and we may not know it yet."

"She's not there. I know it. She found a way to escape, and she's right now trying to either find a safe haven to hide or she's licking her wounds to come out and kill the bastards who did this to her." Russo took a deep breath. "You go there right now, find her, and keep me in the loop. And Garrett?"

"Yes, sir?" Garrett closed his eyes to what he knew he wasn't going to like.

"You fuck this up and so help me, you'll never be able to find a place to hide from what I'll do to you."

Conrad hadn't expected him to threaten him, but before he could say anything, the line went dead. He threw the cell phone across the room and watched it shatter against the brick fireplace. The fucking cunt was doing nothing but fucking up plans that had been in the works for more than a year. He went to his desk again and called Nestor.

"Get me ready to go to Ohio, and don't fucking forget whatever bug spray you can find to keep the shit-for-brains people that live there away from me."

Nestor said that he would do his best.

"And make arrangements for you to go as well. There isn't any reason for you to be in the lap of luxury when I'm forced to go to some shit hole."

~~~

Her body was sore, but warm. Not an unpleasant hot, just…well, hell, she was snuggly warm. When she tried to move closer to what she thought was the source of her comfort, she was met with a soft groan. Pulling back, she looked into the face of Walker.

"You should really learn to wear nothing to bed. It's much more pleasant when you wake up naked next to me. Well, it is for me anyway." He pulled her back and buried his face in her throat. "You smell like sex."

"I most certainly do not. Let me go." Instead of doing as she had demanded, he licked his tongue where his face had been. "Walker, what are you doing?"

Her voice had gone husky. She knew that he'd heard it as well because he nipped at her tender flesh and then moved his mouth up along her jaw and then to her lower lip. Before she could protest, and she was nearly sure she would have, he kissed her.

His mouth was soft against hers, but demanding. Before she could think to protest, he was seeking entrance to her
~~~

mouth, and she let him in. Her entire body felt his command of her mouth, the way his tongue danced along hers, and most importantly, the way his hands began to touch her seemingly everywhere.

When he rolled her to her back, she knew he was being careful of her. It was a good thing too, because right now all she was feeling was him and what he was doing to her. When he cupped her breast from beneath, she moaned. Before she knew what she was doing, she wrapped her hand around him and pulled his ass closer to her heat.

"I want you."

She wanted him as well and nodded at his statement.

"Are you too hurt for me to taste you?"

"Please," was all she could manage. He made his way down her body. When he reached her belly, his hands moved her shirt up her torso until her bra was exposed. Before she could beg him to take it off her, she felt his thumbs at her nipples and her bra pushed up high.

"I want to taste all of you. But your nipples…Christ, they're calling to me." He took one into his mouth as he held himself up off her. His cock was between her legs and she could feel his length and thickness rubbing her clit. Lynne wrapped her fingers into his hair when he suckled on the tip of her breast. She wanted him there forever. But he had other plans and moved down her body slowly.

Her jeans were suddenly gone. She'd heard some tearing sounds, but wasn't concerned about that at the moment. His tongue was moving inside of her navel, causing her nerve endings to come alive with need. Before she could beg him again to take her, he was sitting on his heels and looking down at her from between her thighs.

"I don't want to hurt you."

She doubted that she'd care, but nodded at him.

"I want to make love to you, but I won't here. Not our first time. I want to bury my cock deep inside of you and never leave."

"What are you waiting for then?"

He chuckled.

"Walker, it would be wonderful if you just did something. I'm really needy right now."

His grin was evil. When he ran his finger along her thigh to her apex and down the other side, she wanted to brain him. But when he got off the bed, she thought about getting up and getting her gun to make him finish her off. The damned man was—

"I want to be naked too." She watched as he unsnapped his pants and pulled the tiny tab of his zipper down slowly. "I want to be able to come on you. Mark you with my cum. Are you all right with that?"

"Come inside of me." She wanted to cry when he shook his head, but was distracted again when he pulled his pants off. His boxer briefs showed her every curve, every vein of his shaft, as well as the small wet stain on the tip of where his cock was.

"I'm going to take off my underwear. When I do, would you lick me clean?"

She nodded, not capable of speech.

"I don't want to come down your throat yet, but I do want to feel your tongue on me."

He took off the briefs and moved toward her, stroking his cock as he went. She sat up slightly and opened her mouth for him. The tip of his cock was so thick she wasn't sure he'd fit, but she took him in and swirled her tongue around him. Christ, he tasted delicious.

Walker rocked into her mouth and she gagged when he touched the back of her throat. But as she got used to his girth, she was able to take more and more of him in. When he pulled away and took a step back, she reached for him.

"No. Christ, you're good." He stroked his cock a few more times as he moved to the bed and settled back on his heels. This time when he touched her, he slid his finger into her pussy and thumbed her clit.

The climax was quick. It took her breath away and made her heart feel as if it had stopped for several seconds. As she was trying to recover from the blast of pleasure, she cried out when he suckled her clit into his mouth.

Her body soared up and over without giving her any warning. Walker continued to eat at her until she thought she'd die from it. Even when she begged him to stop, to let her breathe, he continued. She wondered fleetingly if a person could die from this much pleasure.

Lynne looked down her body and watched him look at her. Even as he slid his hands over her hips and to her pussy, she couldn't seem to tear her eyes from him. When he spread her open, her thighs wide over his shoulders, she watched. When he lifted his head, she thought for sure he was going to take her.

"I want you to come again. Come hard for me so that I can get my fill of you."

She nodded as her juices stained his lips.

"When you come this time, I'm going to come all over this pretty pussy and make you come again."

"Yes, please. Walker, please fuck me. I want to feel your cock inside of me. Please, I'm begging you."

He stared at her for several seconds before he sat up again. "I don't want to hurt you, but I can't resist you." He crawled up her body slowly, nipping at her here and licking her there. Her nipples were suckled as his cock teased her entrance. She wanted to wrap her legs around him and pull him deep, but was reminded of her leg wound when she moved to do so.

Walker took her mouth as he entered her. He was filling her, fully and completely. His tongue, tasting of her, invaded her mouth as his cock did her body. In and out he stroked her until she knew that when he touched her sweet spot again she was going to come.

He tore his mouth away and commanded her to come. She was so close anyway that it was no problem for her to obey. But she when she did, it was as if she came apart for a few seconds then came back together. She grabbed for something to hold onto and felt her nails dig into his chest. Blood pebbled in the tiny cuts, and she found herself wanting to taste it. Leaning up, she licked her tongue along the four tiny cuts and came again.

When Walker threw back his head and roared out, she came again, her body responding to his as if they were one. She felt his cum splash against her womb, felt his cock thicken incredibly. She held him to her throat as he licked at her pounding pulse. And when his teeth sank deep, so deep she knew he'd drawn blood, she came again. This time, she felt her vision narrowed to a pinpoint before she blacked out.

Her very last thought was that this was going to be hard to top. Because she knew deep in the back of her mind that it would never be like this with any other man so long as she lived.

CHAPTER SEVEN

Conrad's plane landed at midnight. He was thankful for that because the place was a dump and he didn't want to think about what it might look like in the light of day. When Nestor finally came around the corner with his luggage, he was glad that he'd told him to come along. He didn't have time for petty stuff like standing in line for the turnstile to give him his things.

"It's about time. What the hell were you doing, letting it go around ten times to see if anyone would steal it?"

Nestor mumbled something about his luggage being last to come off.

"I don't suppose it occurred to you to get mine and bring it to me so that I could take a cab to the hotel instead of waiting here for you to get your things?"

Nestor wisely said nothing. Conrad wasn't happy about being there, but more so, he was pissed that he had to come right now when there was so much he could be doing with all the equipment at his fingertips. This place probably wouldn't have Internet, much less a good connection.

They rode in silence to the hotel. It was really nice, much better than he had expected, but he didn't say that to Nestor as they rode up in the elevator together with the bell boy. Conrad didn't want the aide to think he was doing a good job…it might go to his head. When the man who had brought up their things left, Conrad walked around the room speaking to Nestor to make sure he knew that he wasn't on vacation.

"I might need you in the middle of the night and I don't want to have to wait for hours for you to get here. Make arrangements to be at least within walking distance of this hotel." He didn't even bother unpacking his things because it wasn't his job. "And make sure you hang my suits up now so that they aren't wrinkled."

He looked back when there was no answer and was surprised to see that at some point, Nestor had disappeared. He called out his name twice before he went to the phone and asked the hotel clerk to have the idiot paged. He waited for ten minutes before he was told that no one had come forward with that name.

Conrad was pissed. He hadn't given him permission to leave him, and now he had no idea where he was staying, much less how to get in touch with him. He pulled out his cell and tried to remember if he had Nestor's number or not. Usually, he just picked up his desk phone or shouted for him. This was insubordination as far as he was concerned.

Going to his luggage, he was glad to see that his toiletries were right on top, as well as his pajamas. He knew there was a robe on the back of the bathroom door and opted for the one on the counter that was sealed in plastic. For all he knew, the cleaning lady hadn't done her job well and hadn't taken the dirty one out. He pulled the new one over his naked body.

Conrad didn't like mirrors. He'd gotten a bit chubby over the years in the Bureau and he hated that he no longer had time for exercise. Not that he'd done a whole lot before, but now there simply wasn't time. Of course, he could use the gym in the building, but he didn't want to deal with other people's germs.

He ordered room service and was pleasantly surprised to see that they had a great many things to choose from on the menu this late at night. Of course, before he ordered, he'd had to tell them three times who he was. He wasn't going to take no for an answer and they finally let him order from the regular menu. Conrad told them he was the man in charge of their wellbeing, as well as the right-hand man to the vice president, and that they should be proud to have an American like him in their hotel.

He was just settling down in front of the television when there was a knock at the door. He got up to answer it, not even bothering to close up his robe. Whoever it was had come uninvited and he wasn't going to make himself look good for intruders. It was Nestor.

"Where the hell have you been? I've had to order my own food, and my clothes are getting wrinkled just laying in the suitcase. Get them fixed right now."

The man looked ready to speak, but simply nodded and walked to the bedroom. When he was gone, Conrad sat and waited, trying to think up things to berate the man for when he returned. His list was huge before Nestor came out of the room.

"You should also know that they haven't a clue who I am here. What kind of orders did you give them when you made the arrangements for me to stay here? You did tell them who I was, didn't you?"

"No. You haven't made arrangements with the locals yet, and I wasn't sure they'd welcome you with open arms if you didn't speak to them beforehand." Nestor didn't even look at him as the door was knocked upon. "Your dinner is here now."

Nestor tipped the young man after he'd set everything up. Conrad made a mental note to have Nestor around every time he had to tip someone so he wouldn't have to spend his own money. Not that he didn't have plenty of his own, because keeping the vice president happy had some great perks, but he didn't have to spend it all on this trip.

Nestor was moving toward the door again as Conrad cut into his well-done steak. He thought he was simply showing the other man out, but then he realized that he'd gone out again. Shouting for him didn't work, and he was ready to get up and go after him when his own phone rang. He answered it without bothering to look at the caller ID.

"You there yet?" Jerry had taken the time to call. The bastard. "You should have called me the moment you landed and not had me call you. Do you know what it's like to have to sit around waiting for information to come to you instead of going out and finding it?"

Conrad almost said that he was forever bringing him the information and not him going out and finding anything. But he pushed back his dinner and took several calming breaths. "I only just landed an hour ago and had to get to the hotel. There are things going on here that I'm still trying to sort through." Namely, his disappearing aide, but didn't tell Jerry that. "There was also the matter of me making arrangements with the local yokels so that they wouldn't have a fit because I'm in their town unannounced." He was glad that Nestor had given him that bit of information before leaving again.

"I suppose that would be the best course of action. Where is that cunt now anyway? Do you have any other information than what you had this morning?" He'd told him that he thought that she'd escaped somehow and that was why he was there in that town now.

"No. She might have been in the house like I said, but I'm not sure. She's much too smart for her own good." And his as well, Conrad thought. "I'm going to go to the locals in the morning and see what they have on the house, then go from there. For all I know, they might have found her body by now."

"We won't be that lucky. I don't know why you hired her in the first place. Women have their place, and it's not in an upright position." Jerry laughed at his own joke. "Find her. Then maybe I'll have the chance to show her just what I think she should have done with that mouth of hers rather than speak out of turn."

Conrad hung up after a few more minutes of getting his ass handed to him. Jerry was nothing but thorough when it came to blaming others for things that they may or may not have had anything to do with. Like hiring McCray. She'd been working for the CIA a lot longer than he had.

~~~

Walker watched her sleep. She was lovely to look at awake, but when she was sleeping as soundly as she was right now, she looked positively angelic…which he was reasonably sure she wasn't. He glanced back at the bags he'd opened after she'd lost consciousness. He found himself grinning again at that.

He'd never rendered a woman unconscious before. They'd been satisfied, yes, but not out cold like she was. He traced his finger down her neck to the bite he'd given her on her shoulder. He had a feeling that she'd be pissed enough to knock him unconscious before all was said and done.

They'd mated, and completely too. Once they'd exchanged blood, she was as much his as he was hers. And there would be no going back now, no matter how mad Khan
~~~

would be. And he would be too. His parents, however, would be thrilled beyond words.

When Caitlynne stirred, he watched her eyes flutter open and her face light in recognition. She didn't move as her smile went from a frown to looking at him as if he'd committed some heinous act. When she started to sit up, she lay back down quickly, and he reached for her wrist. He had a chance to feel that her pulse was strong if only a little fast before she jerked her hand away.

"What are you still doing here? I thought you would be gone when I woke up."

He shook his head and started to tell her he didn't have a way to get away even if he wanted to when she spoke again.

"I will make arrangements to replace your truck as soon as I get up. Don't you have anywhere you're supposed to be?"

"No, not right now." He ran his fingers over the curve of her breast that the sheet wasn't covering. "We could make love again if you want. I know that I would certainly like to. You're very delicious."

She moaned when he licked the same path that his fingers had taken, only to have his head jerked up when she grabbed a handful of his hair. He wanted more than anything to kiss her, but was sure he'd lose his lip. She looked positively pissed.

"We have to set the record straight right now. You were at my house at the wrong time and I used you. Just like I used you to be fucked. You don't mean anything to me, and in order to—"

He covered her with his body and rocked into her. She was tight and wet, and Walker decided that there had been enough talk. He wanted action. Besides, he could smell her need as sharply as his own.

When she begged him, saying please to him, he rocked again, this time harder and deeper. When her uninjured leg wrapped around his calf, he took her hands and put them above her head as he nuzzled her breast.

"Your skin tastes like manna to me." He took her pert nipple into his mouth and suckled it hard. Then he dipped his head to the other one, giving it the same treatment.

"You have to stop this. This isn't going to get us to the point where you're gone and I can move on." He might have believed her except for the fact that he could feel her sheath as it milked him. She was as close to coming as he was.

Slowly, he moved in and out until he could feel the sweat running down his spine. His balls were tight against his body, and he knew that once she tightened around him he was going to release in her again. This time, he wanted her to bite him.

"Do you have any idea how much you mean to me?" Her head rolled from side to side. "I want to feel you sink your teeth into me, Caitlynne. I want to feel you bite me."

"I can't do that. You're…Christ, yes that feels good. Please, Walker, finish me." He nipped at her throat and she gave him all of it. "You bit me before. Why?"

He nipped again and raised his head. "Bite me, Caitlynne. Please, I want to feel you bite me hard enough to draw blood." He lowered his head to hers and he felt her breath on his neck. Every part of his body screamed at her to finish, and his cat ran along his skin so close to the surface that he felt his claws break through.

She pulled her head back and looked up at him. "What was that?"

He kissed her so that he could take her again before he had to answer questions. When he lifted his head this time, she looked at his throat and licked her lips. "Do it." When he lowered his head this time, she nipped at him. Before he could command her again, she bit.

His cock jettisoned deep and his toes curled as he held her to him. Pounding in her now, he knew she had come, and when she screamed out again, he took her mouth and tasted his blood on her. They were one now. Truly one.

Dropping on her and rolling her so that she covered him, he lay there thinking of all that would come to them as a couple. He knew that by law, he should have told her before he'd taken her blood, but she had been so hot and delicious that he couldn't help himself. He held her for several minutes before he spoke. It was a lot easier for him to talk to her when she wasn't looking at him.

"I'm not really what you think I am. I'm not…I'm not fully human."

She giggled, and he started to ask her why when she spoke. "I don't know, Walker. You felt pretty human to me just now and last night. I was thinking last night that no man would ever be able to give me the same satisfaction as—"

He rolled her to her back and held her down. "No man will ever touch what is mine." His beast had surfaced and wanted to punish her for even thinking there would be anyone else. Walker tried to calm him by telling him she didn't know any better when he was suddenly on the floor and she was sitting up in bed.

"You don't own me. No one does. And get this, big boy, the sex was good, damned good, but I can have that anytime I want, with whomever I want, however I fucking want it." He stood up and started for her, but then he saw the gun in her hand.

He stopped and raised his hands in surrender. "I won't hurt you." He winced when he saw that he'd bitten her again and had not sealed up the wound. Blood tickled down her shoulder and over her bare breast. He wanted to drop down and beg her to let him taste her again. If nothing else, she'd have to let him seal that up. He'd have to do that before they left.

She stood up and staggered slightly. The only reason he didn't try to catch her was because of the gun that never wavered. Not even slightly.

"You have to listen to me. You can't hang around me any longer. The man who I'm running from has a lot of pull. He'll kill you if he thinks it will matter to me."

"Will it?" He knew he'd caught her off guard, so he asked her again as he pulled on his briefs. "Will it matter to you if he gets to you through me, Caitlynne?"

"You've no idea what sort of person I am. I make my living by doing things that good men like you would never do." She sat on the edge of the bed and tossed the gun on it beside her. "Walker, what the hell happened when you yelled at me?"

He sat on the chair and decided that it was now or never. He reached over, picked up the gun, and put it into the bag that he'd opened earlier. There was no sense in pushing his luck.

"The night that my family found you, what do you remember?"

She shook her head.

"Do you remember the panther that found you?"

"Yes. He was big and black. He looked at me like he knew just what I was…how did you know that?"

"He's my dad. And when I came to find you when my mom said you'd saved Dad, I looked for you as a panther as well." She snorted and he continued. "My entire family are werepanthers. And my brother, Khan, became our leader when my dad retired."

"Right. And I'm Tinkerbell."

She lay back on the bed, and he found he wanted to join her there so badly that he had to adjust his cock twice so he wouldn't hurt himself. He realized she was speaking and tried to calm his throbbing cock.

"You don't really believe that, do you? I mean, seriously. Who believes that sort of shit? No one, I'll tell you, no one."

"Would you like to see him?"

She only stared at him as he stood up.

"Don't run from me, Caitlynne. If you do, I will chase you down and bring you back here." He was glad now that he'd pulled on his boxers and not his pants. He slipped them off and let his cat take him. Walker loved to shift. It didn't matter if it was from human to cat or the other way around. The feeling of the change was what he loved. The cat moved along his skin like he was going to consume him, and when he did, he had to blink several times to make his non-human eyes see Caitlynne.

She hadn't moved, for which he was grateful. He didn't want to have to chase her, but he would have if she had left. He leapt up on the bed and lay beside her. She didn't move, not even when he licked her arm.

"Okay, don't be fresh. I'm still…mother fuck. You're really a panther." Walker moved closer to her and put his head on her lap. When she reached her shaky hand out and caressed the top of his head, he purred for her.

Neither of them moved for several minutes. He could see her well, but he knew when she turned her head she was going to say something he wasn't going to like. He moved up her body carefully, trying not to scratch her with his claws.

"This doesn't change much. I'm still a gunman for the government." She turned back to look at him. "I'm working for the government as a hit man. I've been doing it for a long time, and I like it. And I'm damned good at it. I don't just kill people, though that's something that happens more often than not, but I also infiltrate computers, companies, as well as bank accounts. Do you understand what I'm telling you?"

He growled low and licked her arm again. When he was off the bed, he let his human side take him back. Shaking his hair out, he started for the bed and her. She started for the other side when he grabbed her leg and held her. "You aren't going anywhere without me. I didn't tell you this before I shifted, but you're my mate. Do you know what that means?"

"You can't be serious. You think I'm going to be your little cat bitch? Think again, bucko. I'm just plain old human Lynne McCray." He pulled her toward him when she struggled to get away. "Let me go, you overgrown ass. I've got to get out of here before I'm found with you."

"No." He waited for her to calm down and when she did, he wasn't fooled when she stilled. "You're my mate, which means where you go, I go. And I can find you anywhere because I have your scent now."

CHAPTER EIGHT

The little town was shit. There wasn't a single car, including the police vehicles that he'd not be caught dead in. But he had to play nice with the locals or they'd stop him at every turn. He was smiling at the dumbass that was showing him a dead fish that was hanging on the wall when he thought of McCray living in this town.

She'd hate it too, he would think. More than that, she would have turned her nose up at it. He had always imagined her to be high maintenance and not a little bit on the snob side. Conrad had never liked McCray, but he had thought of her often.

"You can go on over to the house if you want, but there isn't anything much left of it to show you." The chief of police, Terrence Palmer, took him out to his cruiser and held the door open for him. Conrad looked over at Nestor, who smiled and climbed into the back seat when that door had been opened.

"It's a far piece to walk if you want. Plus, there are the dogs. Lynne's neighbors said they would protect anyone from strangers, but you don't know the mind of a dog now, do you?"

They were finally moving when Conrad asked a question. "You didn't find any bodies in the house? I don't know where she'd be if she wasn't in there." The chief looked at him oddly, and Conrad tried to think what he'd said wrong. "I mean, she had to be home. She was on leave from what I've heard."

"Leave? I don't know about that. She wasn't home much lately. Said she was working late at the local school. Never saw a woman more dedicated to teaching as she was."

Conrad winced. He'd forgotten that she was a teacher. He glared at Nestor when he didn't so much as look his way. The man was supposed to keep him straight. How the hell was he supposed to remember all the shit that went on in the office? He had better things to do.

"Yes. She is good at her job." He looked out the front window when the chief nodded. "Christ."

The house wasn't just blown up, but leveled. He hadn't been able to see it from the view of the cameras for the simple reason that the explosion had taken them out. There was debris in both the empty lots on either side of her house as well as all over the yards of the people across the street. When the cruiser stopped, Conrad got out with the rest of them.

"Can't tell yet who, if anyone, was in the house when it went up. We're thinking she wasn't home yet. Been collecting her mail for a few days now, and she usually comes on by and picks it up before she heads home again. It's going to be quite a shock to her when she comes back, yes sir it will." He pointed toward the other row of houses about half a mile back. "That's where we found the man. He'd been on her porch near as we can tell, 'cause if he'd been inside, he'd be in pieces and not just broken up."

"Broken up?" Both of them looked at Nestor when he spoke. "What do you mean, 'broken up?' He didn't get burned up, did he?"

"Nah. We figured he was coming across the yard toward the house when he was thrown to the other house, his body hitting the wall over there. Broke near every bone in his body, including his head. Brain nearly spilled out all the way before we was able to get him out of the pool."

Conrad willed Nestor not to ask, but he did. "You mean to say he was imbedded in the pool? As in, a part of it?"

"Yeap. He was nearly flush with the cement bottom when we had to peel him out. Don't know how much longer he would have been there if the Millers hadn't have left a day or two late for their yearly visit to their daughter's. The missus looked out the window and saw him laying there and started screaming bloody murder." Terrence laughed at his own joke. "Course he was, wasn't he? Murdered, I mean."

Every drop of blood in Conrad's body froze. He looked at the cop, trying to ascertain what he knew or what he thought he knew. A glance at his aide told him he was on his own with this one.

"Murdered? I just heard on the report that it was a major gas leak. That there was such a buildup of gas in her house that it blew." The cop nodded. "Then what do you know that they don't?"

"Don't know nothing for sure. Just my own brand of theories. Nice girl like her, what does she do for a living that makes her be able to afford that big old truck of hers? Expensive too. Then there are the long periods of time that she was gone. Days on end." The cop smiled again. "I don't think whatever she does in on the illegal side of the law, it's just that…well…." He reached into his pocket and pulled out a folded paper. "Got this the day they showed up to look around. Says there that the government was investigating this and we were to stay out. Didn't like it much at first, but I let them go on. Like that girl, we all do, and wanted some justice for her house. Now you show up acting like you're just another Joe Blow and asking the same questions."

Conrad figured out two things in that moment. The cop wasn't nearly as stupid as he'd first thought or even hoped he'd be, and he knew more than any of the others, including himself, about what McCray was and what she did for them. He tried to laugh it off, but even to his own ears, he sounded manic.

Killing the cop came to mind. He was reaching for his gun in the holster under his jacket when he saw two more cruisers pull up. When Terrence reached under his jacket and took his gun from him, Conrad knew better than to try to fight him. He looked at Nestor, and he was being disarmed as well.

"You should know that I work for the government and I have the right to carry that. I'm going to get it back." He wanted to strangle the cop when he grinned and nodded. "You're going to lose your job over this."

"Doubtful. You see, I work for the government too. Chief of police might not be as exalted as you seem to think you might be, but I uphold the law same…well, I was gonna say same as you, but I'm thinking you don't." He handed off the gun to the officer standing just behind him. "You see, there are rules. You broke them when you showed up in my town without notice. Then you are carrying a gun you didn't tell me you had. On top of the fact that I just plain don't like you. Now. This is how this here is going to work. I'm going to take you back to the office and you're going to tell me what the fuck—pardon my language—you think you're doing in my town."

Conrad stared at him. The man had balls, he'd give him that. Before he could comment or tell the man that he was wrong, dead wrong, there was a gun at the back of his head. Slowly, he raised his hands until the gun no longer felt as if it was embedded in his skull rather just resting there.

"You've made a serious mistake. Do you know who I am?"

The cop nodded, and the gun banged him slightly.

"You're going to regret this more than you can—"

"Not as much as you are." He nodded and the man behind him jerked his arms behind him. "You should have followed your own rules there, buddy. Right now, you're going to be sitting in my jail cell until someone comes for you or sends me written word that you're okay to let loose. But not before I tell them what a nasty piece of dung you are."

Conrad was shoved in the back of the chief's cruiser, and he noticed that Nestor was put in another one. Someone was going to pay for this, and he hoped the hell he got to be a part of the payback. He started to tell the man driving that he was with the CIA when the man turned and looked at him.

"You say a word, one word, and I have full permission to let you go in the woods yonder and let the big cats have at you. You should know that one or more of them owes me a huge favor." Conrad didn't speak, and the driver turned back to the front.

Cats owed him a favor? And who gave him permission to let him go that way? Conrad looked out the window and watched as the biggest cat (he was sure it was a panther) he'd ever seen came out of the woods and sat watching him. When he nodded at him, it was all Conrad could do not to piss himself. It looked as if the monster was smiling at him.

Conrad let that image keep him company all the way to the jail and in the cell. He knew that others were talking to him, but his mind was too busy working through what he had seen. By the time they had come to bring him dinner, he had convinced himself that he'd seen nothing but a large house cat. Those animals were so stupid they didn't know if they needed to smile or run for the woods. It was time to make his phone call. And he knew just who he had to call.

~~~

George walked into the house and nearly turned around again. Khan looked like he could and probably would bite a nail in two, then swallow it for good measure. He smiled at Corrine, the love of his life, and sat down.

"Where the hell have you been? I've been trying to reach you all damned morning."

George nodded.

"What the hell is that supposed to mean?"

George suddenly snapped. Khan may be leader of this family, but he was still his father. He stood up and shoved his son against the counter. When he started to stand, George hit him in the chest with his fist. "Stay right there. You may be in charge, but I'm still your father, you overgrown shit for brains. I go where I want and do what I need to keep my family safe. If you got your head out of your ass for ten minutes, you'd see that Walker is going to be with this woman whether it's here or not. And to be honest, I had hoped you'd see that as well." When Khan opened his mouth, George glared. He might be old, but he was still a mean motherfucker.

"What your father is trying to say is that neither of them had a choice in the matter. What's done is done and the sooner we accept that, the sooner he'll come home." Corrine stood up as she continued. "What Roseann did to you was horrible, but—"
~~~

"He won't bring that human in this house. Not if you want me to remain."

George took a step back.

"I mean it. It's the human or me."

"Khan, you don't—"

Khan cut his mother off quickly. "I do mean it. Humans aren't going to be welcome here. Not so long as there is breath in my body. I will not allow it, and if Walker wants to come back here, he'd better not have his mate with him."

George pulled Corrine back when she started forward to Khan. His heart broke for his son. George nodded once and turned with his mate to walk out of the house. He had to find some way to fix this, and he wasn't sure how.

"He'll do just what he said, won't he? He'd rather break this family up than see that Walker had nothing to do with who his mate is." George held her close as they walked along the path to their own home. "I can't stand this. None of it. George, what are we going to do?"

"I don't know, love. I really don't. I never knew that Khan's heart was so cold that he'd do this to one of his own brothers." George opened the door, and they both went to the back deck to sit. "I'll try and contact Walker again. See what he wants to do."

George went to the kitchen to get his phone. He had asked Terrance to help him out if anyone came looking at the girl's house. He knew after the team that had come out and had left that someone who'd been responsible would come to see too. Terrance had called him last night when he'd heard that some big shot was in town. He had agreed to let him hang around, and now he was glad that he had. The man smelled evil.

"Walker, someone from Washington showed up today to see Lynne's house. He smelled of something that crawled from under a rock."

Corrine nodded and giggled. "Tell him that little man smelled of fear."

He looked sharply at his mate.

"Of course I followed you. Did you really think I wouldn't? You get into entirely too much trouble on your own."

He thought he'd deal with her later and smiled. His son was talking quickly, and he had to slow him down before he understood him. Something about her running off without him.

"She thinks I'm going to leave her just because of what she does. I've told her it's too late for that, that I'm going with her. I want to beat her ass right now." George laughed at the background noise on Walker's end. "I swear to Christ…I have to go, Dad. She needs a lesson in manners and throwing things."

He closed the phone and looked at Corrine. "I believe they've mated. And she sounds like she can hold her own with him. She was using language that I'm sure she didn't hear from a sailor. It's pretty colorful."

"Good. Then maybe she can hold her own with Khan. Because we both know that's what it's going to take. Someone like her to whoop his ass a time or two."

When his phone rang again he answered it with caution. Marc was the one son that he knew could have a level head, and he wasn't surprised when he seemed to be overly calm about what he wanted to know.

"So, Walker is no longer allowed on our land. What do you suppose is going to happen to them now?"

George asked them who.

"Lynne and Walker. I know they can live on their own and all, but I don't want my brother to not have any contact with me. Nor do Sebastian and Dylan."

"And Reed, what does he think about all this? Is he siding with Walker? Or hasn't he made up his mind yet?"

"Can't find him. He said he was going to get answers and left here before I could talk to Khan. I guess he heard the argument at the house and confronted Khan after you left. I'm not sure what happened, but Khan is nursing a bloodied lip and Reed was limping. But if the dining room is any indication, I would say that they had a few words and they aren't in agreement."

George threw back his head and laughed. Reed was the baby, but he had learned to fight dirty. Having five older brothers had given him that much. Plus, the boy just didn't know when to give up. He handed the phone to his mother when she asked.

"Yes, dear. Your father and I would like to be kept in the loop." She paused for several minutes. "Oh, I like that idea. Yes, I do. Let us know what we can do to help."

She closed the phone and handed it back to him. Before he could ask what was going on, the phone rang again. This time, the number was unknown. The person started talking even before he could say hello.

"Will you please tell your moronic son that I don't care if he's Godzilla himself, he is not strong enough to go with me when I hunt the fucktard down that made me blow up my own fucking house? I swear to Christ, he's more stubborn than I am."

George started to laugh, but held off. The woman was pissed enough as it was. "I'm assuming this is Caitlynne McCray, or is it Bowen now?"

"It's McCray, thanks. Why would you…? I see, it's one of those panther things. Once you fuck someone, every other panther knows. Do I have to be careful of the zoo now?"

George laughed, unable to help himself. "No, the zoo should be fine for you. I'd avoid the wolf cages, as well as the smaller animal cages, though. They can smell him on you, and you know all about cats and dogs."

"Right. You really don't think I visit the zoo, do you?" She took a deep breath. "I sort of accidentally knocked him out. Do you know how long he'll be down? I have to get going."

Her scream had him jerking the phone from his ear. He assumed that Walker was awake now. They were fighting, and he wished he was there to cheer the girl on. When he heard someone cry out, this time he was sure it was Walker. Damn, but that girl was going to do just fine. Suddenly, she was back on the phone.

"I swear to Christ…come here and get him. I can't…what the hell is wrong with him anyway? Doesn't he get that I'm going to get him killed?"

George thought maybe he didn't. He asked her where she was, and when she told him, he told her he'd be there soon. He looked at his mate and asked her what to do now. He handed her the phone when she reached for it.

"Hello, Khan. This is your mother. I need to borrow the SUV, please. And I want you to stay out of my way when I come to get it." She paused. "I don't want you to come with me. I'm quite capable of going to pick up Walker all—no. I forbid you to…suit yourself then."

He stared at her for several seconds. "Why you sly devil you. You did that on purpose. You knew he'd come with…what's he going to do when we get there and Lynne is still with him?"

“He said she couldn’t come on the property. He didn’t say anything about him going to where she is.” She stood up. “Come on and try to act a little more fragile, please. We want him to have to help with Walker, don’t we?”

CHAPTER NINE

Walker glared at her again. The nerve of her…. "I want you to uncuff me right this minute. I will not be sitting here like this when my father shows up."

She ignored him as she'd done for the past hour. He watched her as she packed up her bags. She'd checked every gun in her bag and then refolded her underwear twice. He knew she was trying to piss him off, and he was really going to beat her ass when he got loose.

"You can sit there for five more minutes. Your mother, a very nice woman, by the way, said they'd be here soon." She sat on the bed in front of him. "You know this is for the best, Walker. We can't be seen together or he'll go after you."

He wanted to roar at her, but didn't. The car pulling up out front made him think his dad had borrowed the bigger van to bring him home. He jerked at the handcuffs again. The knock at the door had him glaring at Caitlynne again when she opened it up.

Khan stood there for several seconds, just looking around the room. Caitlynne stepped back, and still he didn't move. Walker looked around the room, seeing it for the first time.

The bed was broken; the mattress was tossed off its frame. The pictures were hanging crookedly, and there were parts of broken frames everywhere. He could see the shower curtain was torn off most of its hooks, and the toilet seat was broken. He looked at his mom when she laughed.

"Good sex? Or did she have trouble convincing you that you aren't going with her?"

Walker flushed, and his dad walked in the room with a whistle.

"Both. Hello, Mrs. Bowen. Thanks for coming and getting him. He's a bit—"

"You did this to her?" Khan thundered toward him when suddenly Caitlynne was in front of him. "Get out of my way, human. I've no—"

Khan ended up on the floor on his back, and Caitlynne held a gun to his head. "Move and I'll shoot you. I'm fucking sick and tired of you treating me like I'm some piece of slime you had on your shoe."

"Don't kill him, dear. You have enough of a mess to explain."

Walker looked at his mom when she spoke.

"Come on, Khan. Tell the nice girl you're sorry she kicked your butt, and we'll take Walker home with us."

"I'm not going anywhere she isn't. I've told her this several times and…would you mind getting off my brother? My cat wants to kill him for touching you."

Caitlynne looked at all of them before she turned to look at him. She didn't look very happy, and he didn't blame her. This had not gone as he had hoped it would. She moved off Khan slowly and never moved her gun off his head. When she stood, Walker noticed the blood on her leg and the large stain on her thigh. She'd opened her wounds again.

"Let me go, Caitlynne. I have to see to your wounds." He heard a noise and started to turn toward it when he was suddenly on the floor and Khan was being held down by Caitlynne.

"Damn it, I told you he'd find me." She took out another gun and handed it to Khan. "You know how to use this?"

"Yes, but why should I care about your ass? You're the reason this is happening." He handed her back the gun and started to stand. She knocked him to the floor again. This time Khan fought back.

Walker didn't know how he was suddenly out of the chair, nor did he remember shifting, but he and Khan were going at each other like one of them was going to die. And Walker was just pissed enough to not care that this was his brother. The sharp pain in his leg had him turn to the source. He stood very still while he watched Caitlynne stand with a gun on them both. He hadn't even heard the report, and that's when he realized that she had a silencer on the big thing. Khan growled low and started toward her when she shot him in the leg as well.

"Now, here is how this is going to work. I'm tired of fucking with you people. I never wanted this. All I did was take some time off my job so that I could recoup from something that should never have gone down. In that time since, I've found out that my boss really is a prick and a liar, there are werepanthers in the world, and one of them hates me more than I do myself." She shrugged. "But that's beside the point. I'm going to go out that door, and if any one of you even peek your face out, I'm going to blow it off. Understand me?" No one moved as she pointed the gun at their heads. "I know you can fucking understand me; that man over there did when I didn't want him to get hurt. So fucking answer me."

Khan snarled, so she shot him again. She must have figured out that they healed quickly. Her next statement confirmed it.

"I know you won't die from this because that man took one to the gut and he's walking around like he's never been sick a day in his life. But I'm reasonably sure that if I shot you in the fucking head, there won't be any recovering from that."

"No, my dear, they won't. But I would like to point out that you're bleeding again and quite badly." His mom stood and moved to her slowly as she spoke softly. "I would like to speak to you, if you wouldn't mind so much. There are things you need to know as well. Especially about Walker and you."

"There is no Walker and I. That's what I've been saying." She swayed a bit, and Walker let his cat go so he could shift. Caitlynne started toward the door as he grabbed up his boxers and moved after her slowly. The wound in his leg was just beginning to heal and still hurt badly, but she was much more important at the moment. She didn't even get to the door before she fell back in his arms.

~~~

"Found her. She's at a hotel on Route Forty. She is there with some man, but we don't know who he is just yet," Nestor said as he walked into the hotel room. "She has her truck and not much else. They went in to get her without my permission and there were shots fired. I'm not sure why the locals haven't shown up yet, but that's about all I have. What do you want me to do?"

They'd been back from the jail for just under two hours. Conrad had taken two showers and had used an entire bar of soap and all the shampoo he'd packed. Nestor had been out getting him more and tossed the bag from the downstairs gift shop. Conrad took the things, pulled out the alcohol wipes,
~~~

and began wiping down his watch, phone, and keys while he thought of what he wanted done now that they had her.

"Where the fuck do you keep finding these morons? Do you make them understand that we are in charge? Do you have someone on her? It would really suck for you if she left."

Nestor said that he had two men on her.

"Good. When do you go back and help?"

"Help? I thought you needed me here. There are men on her much better at keeping her in their sights than I would be, and they know that I'm in charge."

Conrad turned to Nestor and laughed.

"I don't understand."

"Of course you don't. But that debacle that happened yesterday and now today, that was all *your* fault. Had you taken the time to notify that fucking cop, we would never have had to call the president and have him tell the cocksucker to let us go. Then you have people looking for the bitch that don't know what 'under surveillance' means. Christ, you made us look bad and for that…well, you might hold onto your job better if you simply leave right now."

He looked as if he was going to say something, but he only nodded. Conrad was disappointed in the man. He'd hoped for some sort of comment; anything at all would have made him happy because he would have gotten to kill him. He sat down and tried hard not to think about the call he'd made yesterday when Jerry hadn't answered him. He'd had to call the president.

"I need you to bail me out, sir. The locals here are upset because they weren't notified when I arrived in town yesterday. They took my gun, as well as my badge, and said that until someone came to collect me or paid my bail, I was stuck here. And as you have sent me here to find McCray, I can't very well do that from a jail cell."

He'd spoken fast because he had been told numerous times that he had ten minutes to use the phone. Conrad kept an eye on his watch, figuring that they'd cheat him out of minutes if he didn't. He realized that a full minute had gone by without the president speaking. He nearly said his name when he spoke.

"You go to a town that has had a major explosion without notifying the local police that you're in town. You get arrested, disarmed, and your badge, your government credentials, taken away, and then you call me to bail you out."

Conrad closed his eyes as Warren continued.

"What kind of stupid are you? I mean, you're in charge of what I had thought was an elite group of men and women. But with this…well, this kind of stupidity, I can only think that you might not be the man I thought you were. Or maybe you are. Which is it, Garrett? You man enough to do this job? Or should I get McCray to do it for you?"

"No, sir. I'm doing the job just fucking fine. And now I need your help to do what you sent me here to do. Though why you should think a cunt like her can do anything beyond fucking anything that moves is beyond me. She has no respect for me and my position, she makes up shit about the vice president, and for whatever reason, you believed her. And now I'm stuck here. Are you going to help me or not?" He had snapped before he thought. And now he was going to be left there, as he had predicted.

"You listen to me, you little motherfucker. I make the rules and you do them. If I send you to ground zero to find her, you will do it. As for your little problem in Ohio, you'll get out, but not before I'm ready to let you out. While you're sitting there waiting I want you to think of this." Warren took several audible breaths before he continued in that low, frightening tone. "I know a great deal more about all of this shit you're involved in with Jerry than either one of you can know. You will go down with him. Bank on it."

The line had gone dead, and five hours later he and Nestor were let go. Conrad was sure it might have been a good deal longer, maybe even weeks longer, but he wanted him to find his girl, as he'd called her over the past several weeks. When he saw on the receipt that his fine had been paid, it had a time stamp of ten minutes after talking to the man. He had paid and had the cock-sucking cop hold him until then. Conrad stood up when a knock came to the door.

The bellman took his luggage and waited for him to follow. There had been a message when he'd returned that he was to vacate the premises immediately or else. And he had to pay for the room with his own credit card because his government one didn't go through. If the bastard had taken away his clearances, he knew for sure that both he and the vice president were so fucked.

As he was being driven away, his phone rang. He saw it was Nestor and almost didn't answer it. The man was driving him crazy and knew that as soon as he got back to DC he was getting rid of him. Permanently.

"She's gone. When I got back here, she was gone, and the other agents you sent to watch her were in the coffee shop across the street. They said they were ordered to stand down."

Conrad had the driver pull over and close the window between them. "Start from the beginning. What do you mean they were ordered to stand down? I give the orders around here. Who the fuck did they say told them to do that?"

It took Nestor long enough to answer that he knew who it was before he answered. "The President of the United States,

Warren Russo. They said he called them directly and told them that the mission they were on was not something he had sanctioned. That they were to go have a cup of coffee and lunch on him and he'd see them when they returned. They're going back to the White House when they leave here, in Air Force One."

Conrad was fucked. He opened the door to the limo and stood on the side of the road just trying to get his racing heart under control and to try to think. The president probably didn't know the whole story, but if he kept on searching he would soon enough. He realized that Nestor was speaking when he saw his driver get out of the car.

"…I'm to come back too. In the same plane. He told those other agents that McCray was under his care and that he'd get someone to watch over her that she knew and trusted. Do you think he knows anything?"

Conrad nodded at the driver when he indicated with his hands, "What gives?"

"I'm on my way back to explain everything to him."

Like hell, Conrad thought.

"As soon as I get it cleared up, things will be fine. You just do as I tell you and I'll take care of the rest. And, Nestor, you say a fucking word about what you know and you'll be going down with me."

Nestor said he understood, and they hung up. Conrad got into the limo again and decided that he was fucked no matter what and had to make plans. One of them was to not go back to DC. He was as good as dead if he did. As soon as the limo pulled up in front of the airport, Conrad knew he had to make other arrangements. There were five men standing there waiting for him when he got out.

"Conrad Alan Garrett? We're to escort you to the plane and stay with you until it takes off. Do you have anything that needs to be taken out of your bags before we get to the terminal?"

"No. My weapon. But no, nothing else. I do have to use the facilities. Would that be possible?" He didn't think they were going to let him, but he was escorted there and left to use the stall on his own after they took his service weapon. One of them stood just on the other side of the stall door and he knew that one or more of the other agents were keeping anyone from coming in. Conrad knew he was going to go to prison and didn't know if he could survive it.

He sent two text messages out and heard from both men. He smiled as he took out the battery to his phone and broke it in half. Flushing the pieces down the toilet had him nearly cry out when they didn't seem to want to go, but after the second try, they disappeared. He was as ready as he would ever be.

He pulled the gun out of his ankle holster and pointed it at the man he knew was probably standing close enough for him to shoot and kill. Chuckling slightly to himself, he mouthed the word, "Bang." Before he could change his mind he put the gun to his chin and pulled the trigger.

CHAPTER TEN

Lynne woke, but didn't move. She was trying to get her bearings when a sudden flare of light had her turn away from it. She heard someone mumble, "Sorry," and it was dimmed somewhat. When she looked, whoever it was had put a towel or something over it.

"I repaired your wounds, though they're healing a good deal faster than previously. The one in your shoulder is nearly closed and the ones in your leg are doing much better. But there is still the matter of your loss of blood. You're going to be weak."

She sat up and stretched her arms over her head. Her nakedness didn't bother her, but it apparently did Walker. His low growl made her tingle all over, but she tried not to let it bother her…*tried* being the operative word.

"Where am I? I don't believe this is a hospital, it's too homey. Am I at your parents' house again?"

"No. This is mine. I have a clinic in the basement I use for the paranormals to come to if they want." He took the cover off the lamp and she could see him better. "You and I will need to talk. There are things I've not had the opportunity to explain to you, and I apologize."

"You can start by telling me why the sudden heal factor? Is it because you think we're mates or whatever? And so you know, I'm coming back to the other 'paranormals' comment. I'm assuming that means there are more than cats." He nodded. "I can't be your mate any more than I can shift into something. Hell, it would be more likely for me to wear a dress, and that so isn't going to happen."

"My blood is mixed with yours. When we exchanged blood, that made you have some of my healing powers. I would guess that you'll be a little stronger as well, though the thought of you being stronger frightens me a little."

She knew he was trying for a joke, but she wasn't in the mood for it. She tossed the covers off to find that her ankle was shackled to the bed. She didn't mind. She knew that if she wanted to it would be as simple as a walk in the park for her to open it. Every agent and cop worth their salt had a hidey key on them somewhere, so she simply lay back on the hospital type bed and covered back up. "You can't keep me here. You know that, right?" Again, he nodded. "Well, how about if we get this thing done so I can get out of here."

"All right. First, you are my mate. When I followed your blood when you were first hurt I knew who you were to me. According to legend, there is only one mate to each of us and sometimes, as now, they aren't always the same as us." She didn't say anything as he continued. "Also, and I know this part is somewhat screwed up, I'm supposed to protect you at all costs. Though lately, I'm thinking it might be the other way around."

"What happens if I say no? What if I said I don't want you?" He shook his head, but before he could answer her she continued. "There has to be some sort of clause that says one or both of us can get out of this. I mean, what if we really hate each other?"

"Not possible. We may start out not liking each other overly much, but we get there in the end." He grinned at her. "And the sex is phenomenal."

When he moved to the bed to touch her, Lynne didn't comment. Cats liked to be touched, she knew, and apparently so did werepanthers. She thought it best if she didn't let him touch her, but his skin against hers felt like heaven. Then he laced his fingers into hers and held her.

She wanted him. Right now, and anyway, he wanted her. When his nostrils flared, she knew that he could smell her arousal and pressed her legs together to try and ignore what was happening. It only made matters worse.

"I'm not a person people like you usually hang with. I'm sarcastic, mean at times, and I don't know dick about dating. I did it once or twice and it was boring. When I wanted some sexual relief I either did it myself or found someone to fuck me. No biggie." She shifted on the bed again and pulled at her hand. "You're squeezing me too tight."

He let go immediately. "I'm sorry. But you should know that as my mate, if another man comes near you, I will be ripping his throat out."

She started to make a comment, but only stared at him. Then, when she looked away, he sat down on the edge of the bed. He didn't hurt her again, but he did hold her hand. She spoke softly, but she was sure he could hear her just fine.

"I'm not your usual run-of-the-mill girl, Walker. I go into places others would balk at; I do things that aren't always legal, but part of my job. I've been shot, beat up, and usually left for dead most of the time. And now there's this prick after me that has the backing of some very important people." She turned to look at him. "You'd be better off finding some nice little kitten to be your mate. It will be safer for you all."

He kissed her then, gently and without touching her anywhere else. When she opened her mouth under his, Walker took what she offered him and moaned when his tongue moved along hers. She moaned again when he cupped her breast; her nipple hardened when his thumb brushed over it. The knock at the door made her want to snarl, but it was for the best. For now.

Walker went to the door as he adjusted his cock. Before he opened it, he turned back to her and smiled. He looked like he was telling her this wasn't finished, and she wanted to tell him hell no it wasn't, but he opened the door before she could beg him not to.

"I'm sorry, Doctor Bowen, but this just came for Miss Bowen. The man said he has to wait for her signature."

Everything in her froze when she realized what the nurse said. "Who is it? What does he look like?" She tossed off the covers and looked for her clothes. "Where the fuck are my clothes? I have to see who that is."

Walker didn't argue with her, though she expected him to. He reached into a drawer and handed her a pair of sweat pants and an oversized t-shirt. She knew as soon as she slipped the shirt over her head it was his. When she asked for her other bag, he nodded to the small closet and closed the door on the nurse, asking her to wait. He took the cuff off her ankle as she pulled her hair back into a sloppy ponytail.

"What's going on? Why are you running around here like—?"

"Someone knows where I am. That can't be good. Because unless you took out an ad in the paper, no one should know that the two of us have had any contact." She checked her weapon and put it in the back of the pants. Its weight pulled at them, but there was no help for it.

Walker reached in the bag and took out another handgun. “I can use this. I hope to Christ I don’t have to, but I can. Also, I’ve contacted the others. My brothers are on their way here in the event there might be trouble.” She nodded at him. “Caitlynne, I don’t suppose if I asked you to not go up there you’d do it, would you?”

She didn’t answer, but went to the door. The package was in her hand and she felt its weight. Cell phone, she’d guess, but didn’t know for sure. Bombs could be fairly small and cause a great deal of damage.

She jerked open the front door after having some help from Walker in finding her way to the front of the house. It was a big fucking house. The man standing there was someone she knew. It didn’t give her a warm and fuzzy feeling knowing who might have sent him, but she did feel somewhat better.

“Miss, I need a signature for the rest.”

She nodded, but didn’t reach for the large envelope or the clipboard.

“He said you were to take it or he’d come here and give it to you himself.”

She snorted and he smiled. “How did you find me? I’ve been off the grid for some time now and he wasn’t made aware of my moving around.”

He shoved the clipboard at her and the envelope. She signed and handed them back. He smiled again and tipped his hat before slipping her a small folded up piece of paper. After nodding again, he left.

“Is everything all right?”

She turned to look at Walker and three panthers.

“Do you need for one of them to follow him?”

“No. Christ, you guys are huge, aren’t you?” She held the package and envelope to her chest while she looked down at the paper. "I have to make a few calls. I don't want to…this could be bad. Worse if he's involved."

"Who?" She looked over at George and decided that if they wanted in, they were going to get it all. "Who knows you're here?"

"It's from Warren, the president. And from this note, I'd say he's not a happy camper."

~~~

Reed and Sebastian looked ready to get to work. Walker watched them while he fixed lunch for them all. He wasn't happy about the turn of events, but figured if they got this thing over with, he and Caitlynne could get on with their lives. He set the platter of food in front of them and glared when they didn't offer it to Caitlynne first.

"Okay, this is what we have so far. And just so you know, this leaks from this room and I'll be hired to kill you both." The men looked at her, then at him. He was pretty sure she wasn't kidding.

"I'd do what she says. The president didn't seem all that thrilled about her not bringing in real agents to help her. He seemed to think you two didn't know squat about computers."

Reed snorted, and Sebastian sat back and looked at Caitlynne. He was thinking about something profound, no doubt. When Caitlynne looked up at him, they stared across the table for several seconds before Sebastian finally spoke.

"What is it you do? I mean, I know that you work for some initial-based office in the government. And while I don't care, there is something about you that makes me think you're a whole hell of a lot more important to the president than just an analyst. Why would he make sure that you had all this equipment within an hour after asking him for it? What is it exactly that makes you worth all this?"
~~~

Walker wanted to know too. Every time they started to talk about it, something or someone interrupted. He didn't think she was going to answer them when she stood up and moved around the kitchen. There was a file sitting there that no one had touched, but she picked it up now.

"This man is the vice president, as you know." She started pinning pictures to the large board that took up nearly half his wall. "He works for this man and this one." She hung eight more pictures, no longer speaking. When she stepped back, she picked up a magic marker and some index cards. As she wrote, she continued talking and hanging the cards with the pictures.

"Eleven years ago, there was an explosion that killed nine people. Not a lot when you think about how big the explosion was, but the people it killed had information that could help us now. They were Jerry Small's family. All of them. When the rubble was cleared, we discovered there was nothing left. Not a single sheet of paper and no pictures. But what we did find was the incendiary device. It was American made."

"Where was this?" Reed flushed when she grinned at him. "I'm assuming that it was important to someone that it was made here so it only stands to reason that it wasn't in this country."

"It was. But it was put out that it was a terrorist hit. A way to help Small run for a seat he wasn't in the position for now or then. At that time he was running for government office in some sort of leadership position. What it did was get him the sympathy vote, which put him in line for the office of president. But someone was better and he didn't like that, so we think he had him killed too." She walked around the table and picked up another file. "Small was asked to be on the ticket when I told them that he shouldn't be issued any sort of clearance. Now they need my help to figure out what they hadn't before."

"You have that much pull with the president?" Walker shook his head when she nodded at his question. "How? How is that even possible? You said yourself that you're nothing more than a hired gun."

"A hired gun that uncovered the plot that saved everyone in the White House." She moved to the wall again. "This man, Clement James, came to me about two years ago with plans, a layout of the entire building, including all escape hatches and tunnels. He said he'd been given it to come up with a plan to block all of them so that in the event of something going down, no one could come inside and take over."

"He didn't believe them. And I'm guessing neither did you."

She shook her head at Sebastian's statement.

"You told the president, and he took care of it then."

"No. I took care of it because no one would believe an analyst and he knew it. Which was what I was at the time. And before you ask, I'm not telling you how I did it. Suffice it to say, a lot of people were arrested." She pointed to another man. "This is…was Conrad Garrett. He was my boss and in charge of a specialized group of men and women that worked to keep people in line. Mostly it was computer work, much like you two are doing now, but some of it was going in and taking out a target. He killed himself early this morning in a bathroom stall at the airport here in Ohio. He had had words with the president and had pissed him off."

"You killed people."

She nodded at Reed's statement.

"So you really are a hired killer."

"Assassin." She put a line through Garrett's picture. "And this man, even though he's dead, is still having someone work to get me out of the picture. And now, because you people don't listen when I tell you it's dangerous, your family is on that list. And as I have said several hundred times, he won't stop no matter what."

"And now that we're family, we won't either. You have to know that by now too." Sebastian stood up and started to reach for Caitlynne. At the last minute he looked at Walker. Walker nodded and his brother hugged her to him.

"You people really like to touch and hug, don't you?"

Walker noticed that she didn't struggle, and he smiled at her.

"Don't get used to this, big boy. I'm not much of a touchy-feely type of person."

"We'll bring you around." Sebastian stepped back and looked at Reed. "We have to go. We have to go into town and get the rest of the things for family dinner, and I think you two want to be alone."

They left within minutes. Walker didn't move from where he was leaning against the counter. He watched her gather up some of the papers his brothers had left in a mess. When she started straightening the same pile again, he walked up behind her and wrapped his arms around her waist.

"You'll keep them safe. All of us." He kissed her shoulder and then her throat. "You'll see…we're a tough bunch."

"I couldn't keep my partner safe." She'd told him about her partner last night. "He was a very good friend and we worked really well together."

"I know, love." He turned her in his arms and kissed her before continuing. "But we're not human like him. We can keep you safe while you take down this asshole."

"I don't know if I can or not. How will I be able to do my job and keep all of you from being killed too? Do you have any idea…do any of you have any idea what I'm up against? If this person finds me and all of you, he's not going to play around. He's going to hurt me until I beg him to kill me, and then kill me slowly. I've really fucked up his plans."

Plans that she didn't know fully what they were yet. She'd told him that she and her partner were going into what the vice president was using as a meeting house. They had been there to get them all together and take them down when Melvin was killed. The man had taken a bullet meant for her and she'd been captured and beaten pretty badly. She had escaped only because they hadn't expected her to have a second gun. That was why she'd been at home the day the Ingrams had kidnapped her. She believed they were to kill her, but had wanted to have fun first.

Walker's phone went off on the counter. He wanted to ignore it, but he was on call and needed to go when needed. Picking it up, he saw that it was indeed the hospital. He told them he'd be right there. "I have to go. Will you be…?" He laughed. "Of course you will be fine. But when I get back, I expect you to be naked and in the bed. I want to bury myself deep inside of you several times before morning."

"Okay." Her grin made him laugh again. With a quick kiss on her nose, he grabbed up her keys and left. He thought more and more about it being the right time to open his own practice and staying at home more. Of course, he'd probably not get a damned thing done with her there next to him all the time, but it would be worth it.

He frowned when he thought of Khan. He missed his brother something horrible. He wanted to make this right between them, have his brother see that Caitlynne wasn't anything like Roseann had been, but he couldn't do that with his brother avoiding him all the time.

He decided to talk to his mom. She'd know what to do, and she'd make Khan meet with him. Not really the way he wanted to get things going, but he had to do something. Khan and he used to be so very close until Caitlynne. And he wasn't giving her up.

CHAPTER ELEVEN

Jerry threw the book across the cell and looked around for something else to throw. The motherfucking bastard had taken the easy way out. He wished he had Garrett there right now so that he could throw him against the wall as well. Jerry turned when someone started clapping their hands slowly.

"You need more things to toss? I can have it arranged so that you can have some plastic cups brought to you." Russo was looking at the mess as he spoke again. "You can't have any glass, however. I don't want you taking the coward's way out like your partner did."

Jerry stiffened. He hadn't been made aware that Russo knew about him and Garrett, and he stretched his neck to try and buy himself time before answering. It would be just like the man to fish for something he had no idea about. "Partner? What partner? I'm just pissed about being held here when you have no grounds for it. I demand that you let me out of this hell hole so that I can resume my duties." Russo was shaking his head before he finished. "You have nothing on me but what that little cunt gave you before she died."

"McCray isn't dead."

That startled him. Last he'd heard from Garrett was that he was sure she was dead, that the house that had gone up had had her in it. "Good. A girl like her would be a great asset if we needed her for anything in the future."

Russo only laughed.

"You don't believe I had anything to do with her house going up, do you?"

Russo leaned back against the wall. Jerry didn't like the knowing look on his face any more than he did the man himself. He tried to think what had made him look like he'd just won the lotto when he spoke again.

"I didn't tell you her house blew up. Nor do you have any way of hearing about it on the news, and there aren't any newspapers given to you. As far as I know, you have no cell phone, and computer time is limited as well as monitored. So I can only surmise that you have something you shouldn't." He nodded to his left, and suddenly five armed men were there. "These nice gentlemen are going to toss your cell. And you personally if they don't find anything in here. I certainly hope for your sake they don't."

As he walked away, the men opened the cell door. One of them ordered him to strip. He nearly refused, but noticed that the man had his fingers on the trigger. Jerry started to undo his tie. He was going to make them all pay for this, just as soon as he was out of there.

He was led, naked, to another cell. There was nothing in the room but a cot with a thin mattress on it and a blue blanket, as well as a commode that hung on the wall. He looked around and then at the man who still held the gun to his head.

"I can't stay here. This is a prison cell." The man indicated that he sit on the bed, which he did. "I demand that you take me back to my original cell this minute. You aren't going to find anything in there that you didn't—"

"Found his stash."

Jerry looked up at one of the other men who had a large box in his hand. "An iPad, cell phone, and a laptop. There are also a few things that look like they might be video recordings. I'll put them with the other things."

As the gunman backed out of the cell, Jerry realized this was his new digs. He reached over and pulled the blanket, a wool one that had seen better days, to cover his body. He was going to kill that McCray girl as soon as he killed off Russo.

Jerry knew that at that moment his chances of getting out of this cell, or any cell for that matter, were getting pretty slim. He didn't doubt that when they saw the videos they were going to know where he'd gotten them, and that little pisser Nestor was going to be in the cell next to him. He'd been bringing him the information as well as the equipment needed to see beyond the four walls since he'd been put in the other cell so long ago.

He began making a mental list. There were things he knew that no one else knew, and when he'd received the call an hour ago, the woman would be dead within a few days anyway. The one thing that Garrett had done right before he'd killed himself was contact another piece of the puzzle. He'd made arrangements to have her killed, as well as the president. The man may have been a coward, but he had been a smart one.

McCray held the key to him being there. She had information that was going to have him sentenced to certain death by firing squad rather than a long prison sentence. He was sure he knew what it was, but he wasn't positive. She was too untrusting to share that information with Garrett.

She knew or had something that put him there when he'd had his family killed. In fact, he'd been the one who had drugged them all and set fire to the house they were in, burning them alive. If he was really down he'd simply remember their screams…all of them, from his parents to his grandparents, as well as his younger siblings. Jerry had wanted something badly enough not to want them to tell anyone they were related, not to mention all the dirt they had on him.

Jerry lay down on the cot and didn't move when a box was shoved into the room with him. The same man held a gun on him when the door had been opened, and he stood watching him as the box was pushed in. When they were both gone, he got up to see what it was.

Books that he'd never read, but had asked for because he could, a single plastic glass that had a small crack in it, toilet paper, a small hand towel that was marked with a number on it, and last but not least, his iPad. It was shattered and all the insides were stripped out. He simply laid it on the floor and tried not to think about what had been on it.

There was nothing of use to him there, not if he didn't count the necessities. He wondered if he'd get his clothes when he noticed the orange jumpsuit in the bottom of the box. The number on it matched the one on the tiny towel. He thought about refusing to wear it, but thought it would be better than being naked. He had one more thing that they hadn't found and reached to the mattress he'd been sitting on to pull it out. Nestor had told him the cell phone was there months ago, just in case. He told him that he'd hidden one in each cell inside the mattress so that if he ever had to move, he'd be covered. Jerry took it out and turned it on. Time to make things happen.

~~~
~~~

Walker opened the door a little after midnight. He'd been gone for nearly six hours, and he wasn't really surprised to see Caitlynne still sitting at the table working. She looked up at him when he cleared his throat.

"There's something here I can't find. Something that connects the dots that I'm not seeing."

He looked at the large board that was covered from top to bottom, then back at the table. She had three computers running something and a small device hanging out of each one. There were papers everywhere, including the counter a few feet away. He didn't see any plates, only a single glass that had water, but no ice. He would bet she'd not touched it since he left.

"I'm hungry, are you?"

She nodded absently.

"Okay. I need to move some of these things. Will that be all right?"

She didn't answer, but got up to move them to the already overflowing table. She sat back down and looked at the computers again. Smiling, he decided that he'd distract her after he fed her.

He made them simple sandwiches of ham and cheese. She picked off the lettuce and tomato and ate hers in three bites. When she eyed his sandwich, he handed it to her, made himself another one, and gave her a glass of tea. She drank it down in one drink. She was going to be hard to keep filled if this was any indication. He finished his dinner and watched her for a few minutes. When she looked up, he smiled.

"You were supposed to be waiting for me in our room." She looked around as if seeing what she'd been doing for the first time. "You've been too wrapped up in this to remember, I understand."

"You've only been gone what…thirty minutes, forty-five? I only just got a good start on this and now you're back. I thought I'd have more time."

"I've been gone for six hours, love, and you probably haven't moved a bit, have you?" She started to protest, but looked out the window over the sink. "How about we go to bed and maybe after you sleep, you'll find your dots."

"I can't let him harm you guys. It's not right that he can do whatever he wants to me, but I know you guys had nothing to do with any of this."

He nodded and helped her stand.

"You still want to fuck me?"

He laughed. "No. I want to make love to you. Fucking is for strangers. I want to make love to you."

"It's the same thing, Walker. The end result it exactly the same."

He picked her up and started to the stairs.

"I'm quite capable of walking on my own, you know. Besides, I should go back to that hotel and stay there. It would be a lot safer if I—"

"You mention leaving me again and I swear I will beat your ass. The sooner you get it through your thick skull you're mine, the better off things are going to be." He opened the door to his room, realizing that this was the first time she'd been in there. "If you want to change anything, I don't care."

She walked around the room when he put her down.

Walker tried to see the room through her eyes. It was large and full of windows. He loved the outdoors and in the deep of summer, he would open them all and let the earth in. There were times when he would sleep out on the large second floor deck he'd had put on just for that reason.

His bed was huge to accommodate his large frame. Walker was a little over six-foot-five and most mattresses were just too small for him. He was glad that Caitlynne was tall. He wasn't sure what he'd have done if she'd been small.

"It smells like you do." He wondered what she meant when she continued. "I mean very earthy, I guess. Sort of what you'd think of if you camped outside in the summer. I guess that's about right, huh?"

"I smell like that to you as you smell like something similar to me. We have a unique scent to each other that no one else can smell." He sat on the bed as she moved around the room. When she picked up a picture he laughed and told her who they were. "It's all of us when we went to the Smoky Mountains when we were kids. Reed is the baby, and in that picture he's about five. Monster of a kid too."

"I like most of your brothers." She turned to look at him. "Now what?"

He wanted to tell her to come to him, but was sure that wasn't what she meant. "We can start over if you want. The end result will be the same, but it might make it easier on you. I want you. Desperately, but I won't force you into anything. My cat would like a taste of you, mostly to bind with you, but I can control him."

"Taste as in bite me?" He nodded. "I don't know about all that. That part of you has very sharp teeth, and I'm reasonably sure he had big claws too."

He nodded and told her to come to him. He wanted to touch her. She moved slowly as she unbuttoned her blouse. Watching her, he leaned back on the bed and waited for her. He wanted her to make the first move tonight.

The blouse hit the floor when she was only about five feet from him. Her pants, soft lounge pants, were at her hips when she moved up to unclasp her bra. He loved the front closure ones and held his breath as she opened it and it still cupped her breasts.

"What do you taste like, Walker? Is it possible for me to take you into my mouth like you did me?" She pulled off her pants, leaving on her panties that matched her pretty bra. "What if I told you I wanted to go down on you, that I wanted to feel you come down the back of my throat? Would you let me?"

His cock felt strangled in his pants and when she dropped to her knees in front of him, he didn't move. If she wanted to do those things to him, he certainly wasn't going to tell her no. When she ran her hands up his thighs to his hips, he rolled his hips and moaned.

"Touch me, Caitlynne. I want to feel you wrap your hands around me."

She rubbed her cheek over his jeans-covered cock and lifted her head to look at him. He wasn't above begging, but before he could she opened the snap on his jeans. The zipper went down slowly, mostly because his cock was so hard she was having trouble making it over him. When she finally got it down he raised his hips up to help her pull his pants and boxers off completely. He was glad he'd taken off his shoes before coming up here with her.

She stood over him now, his pants in her hands while she stared at him. She started at his chest and moved slowly over his body, seemingly not missing an inch of him. When he felt her eyes on his cock, he reached down and fisted it. It was that or he was going to hurt himself.

"You're hard. Longer than I thought, too, and thick." She licked her lips as she continued. "Taking you down my throat is going to be difficult. But I want to, need to. If I make you come down my throat, will you help me to come too after?"

He answered her with a strangled, “Yes,” and she knelt down again. He nearly came when she gently cupped his balls in her hand and licked them. Christ, he was going to come before she even touched his cock. When she wrapped her mouth around him, he cried out. Christ, he was going to die.

Her mouth was wondrous. She wrapped her tongue around his crown, then sucked hard on it. Her fingers never stopped massaging his balls, and even when they tightened, she didn’t stop. As she licked along the thick vein on his shaft, he cupped the back of her head and drew her mouth back over him.

Every time he felt as if he was going to come, she’d back off. Sweat poured off him, and he was hoarse from begging her to finish him. Over and over she teased and licked him until he was ready to jerk her off him and take her hard. Then she did something that threw him over the edge; she slid her finger into his ass.

He held her over him as he came. Pumping wildly, he knew he was probably hurting her, but couldn’t have stopped if she’d put a gun to his head. His cock emptied in her for what seemed like hours before he lifted his head and looked down at her. A stream of his cum was on her chin, and he felt his cock harden again.

He was wild for her, and his cat wanted his share. Yanking her up over him, he slammed her down over his hard cock and rocked her hips over him. She was wet, soaking wet, and he knew she was close to coming. Throwing her over to her back, he didn’t stop the brutal way he was taking her and lifted her legs up to his shoulder so that he could take her deeper.

She didn’t beg him to stop, but told him harder. He leaned to her throat, his cock so deep he was sure he could touch her womb, and he let his cat go a little. His fangs sharpened and lengthened until he could feel them with his tongue. Caitlynne moved her head and offered him her neck. He sank his teeth deep.

He heard her scream, but she held him to her. Even as he knew he should stop before it was too late, he tore at her flesh. Lapping the blood with his tongue, he grabbed her hips, tilted her tighter to him, and came deep inside of her again. When she came with him, around him, grabbing at his cock with her sheath, he knew what he'd done.

He'd not just let his cat mark her, but he'd changed her. Caitlynne would be cat. That was, if she survived the change. He lifted his head when she went limp. Christ, she was covered in blood. And it wasn't until he pulled away from her that he realized that she'd bitten him too. He moved off the bed and tried to think.

He'd never changed anyone before, but he'd heard that humans as a whole didn't survive it most of the time. He thought he'd read the chances of survival were like three percent. Walker reached for his cell phone as he went to the bathroom and got a washcloth to see how much damage he'd done. Looking in the mirror shocked him.

She'd not just bitten him, but had torn at his throat as well. Deep marks from her teeth were covered in blood as well as where her nails had dug into his chest. Turning, he could see where she'd marked up his back as well. Going back to the bed, his call was answered the same time that Caitlynne moaned.

"Mom? I've…Christ, I didn't mean to. I didn't even…she can't die. I won't allow her to. What do I do?"

His mom was quiet for what seemed to him like hours. When she spoke, he wanted to snarl at her it wasn't funny. The humor in her voice made him think that she'd lost her mind.

"I take it you've gone beyond marking her and you've begun the change. What does she think of this?" She laughed again. "She'll be fine, Walker. Congratulations."

"I don't want to be congratulated for this," he snarled in the phone. "What the hell do I do to stop it? She and I…we were making…Christ, I didn't even know it was going to happen. It just…I…Mom, she doesn't know what to expect. She'll die. Christ, Khan will kill her. Kill us both."

"Now you listen to me, young man. That girl is a lot smarter than you or anyone else gives her credit for. Of course she won't die. I believe she's just too stubborn to let that happen." She took a deep breath. "As for Khan? Don't worry about him. If he doesn't come to accept her, then it'll be his loss. That girl will be fine. Just fine."

"She's not waking up." He flushed when he explained to her that they'd been having sex when it happened. "What do I do to keep her from dying?"

"I'd go and run her a nice bath. She won't be happy to be covered in blood when she wakes. I'm assuming that you bit her hard." He said he had torn at her throat. "Good. That's the best way. Quicker and much easier on you."

He didn't care how easy it was on him, it was her that he was worried about. He told his mom that she had bit him too and she laughed. He thought when this was over, he was having his mother committed. She had lost it.

"She took more of you into her, Walker. It's the best way for her to get through this. Clean her up and keep her warm. In a few hours or less, knowing her, she'll be up and ready to kick your ass for making such a fuss about this."

Christ, he hoped so. He really did.

CHAPTER TWELVE

Warren read the list of things that had been found in Jerry's cell. He was still having trouble wrapping his head around the fact that he had all of it, much less the stuff that had been on most of it. Phone numbers notwithstanding, there was the video of McCray's house going up that had disturbed him the most. The other surveillance videos made him realize that he'd been having her watched for months…almost as long as Jerry had been under arrest.

"We've located Carvey. He's in lockdown. He said he'd give you all you wanted on Garrett if you'd not kill him." Marshall David, his only trusted friend and lover, sat on the big couch and stretched. "He seems to think we might need him alive far more than wc do dead."

"Do you think he has more than this?" He swept his hand over the top of his desk that was covered in files and papers of transcripts that had been found on the phone and iPad they'd found in Jerry's cell. "Most of this stuff here is enough to bury him with the electrodes still attached to his worthless body."

Marshall shrugged. "He claims that Garrett made a few calls before he offed himself. Said he hired a man to take out

Lynne as well as you. Said he knows the name as well as method."

"Do you believe him?"

Again, Marshall shrugged. He knew there was no sense in pushing him. He would get to the point, if he had one, in due time. Warren picked up one of the pictures that had been on the phone and stared at it.

"The Ingrams, the men who took her from her house and beat the shit out of her, were killed execution style. We went to their last known and found them too. They've been dead about two weeks. About the time her house went up. Bullet to the head for them, both hands behind backs, and on their knees best we can tell. Hard to tell with them all wrapped up like they were. Someone, Conrad probably, didn't want them to tell."

Tell what, he wondered, but Marshall continued.

"The explosion is being considered a murder scene. The guy that was killed, he was one of Garrett's too. The man was a sleeper as far as we can tell."

A sleeper. Someone who would go in to do a job and disappear without a print, someone who could walk right by you, shoot you dead, and not be seen. They usually worked at night when their victims were asleep and were never on any books as far as he could tell. While he knew that sometimes they were a necessary force, Warren didn't care for them.

He tossed the picture of McCray and a man who had his back to the camera back on the desk. "I can't bring her in. I don't know what she's planning. I have no idea who the men are she's with other than their names. And I don't know if whatever is going on will be the end of either of us." He looked at Marshall when he laughed.

"You don't really think that she'd tell you the answer to any of those if she was standing right here, do you? Hell, she probably wouldn't tell you if I put a gun to her head. But I can tell you that if I was in a situation like we're in right now, I'd want her just where she is. Because you know as well as I do that whatever happens, she's going to get to the bottom of it."

Warren nodded and stood up and paced around the room. He hated that chair. When Marshall spoke again, he nearly missed a step and fell. He turned to look at him as he continued.

"The people she's with are known to be straight shooters around town. They live on about seven hundred acres of prime wooded land that may or may not be taken from them in a couple of months. The city council is trying to have them give it over for reasons they're not disclosing. But they hint at wanting it for a park, a big one to bring capital to the area. The Bowens aren't going down without a fight, it seems." Marshall grinned. "I've already put some feelers out and had it...delayed until you had a chance to tell me to stop it. There's something else you should know."

Warren sat down. He wasn't going to like this and when Marshall leaned up in his chair and looked him in the eye, he was positive about it. He leaned toward him as well. They could speak low enough that not even the microphones could pick it up.

"They're panthers."

Warren leaned back, then got up to pace again.

"I only just found out about an hour ago. They're not with any other group, but keep to themselves. There are six men, ranging from age twenty-eight to nearly thirty-six. Parents are still around. Walker, the second oldest, is the one that McCray is staying with. From all accounts about him, he's a good man and a great doctor. Has privileges at most of the hospitals in the state. The rest...all have some connection to the area. Two are computer geeks, one is a financial wizard, the oldest is a business owner, and the other works for the local cops. He's said to be too good for the town, but very well liked. All the women have nothing but great things to say about them as well."

He wouldn't doubt that. Warren looked back at his friend. "Does McCray know what they are?"

"Don't know. If she's living with the doc, and it's a pretty clear bet she is, then I would say yes. But with her, it probably doesn't matter." He gave a smile that Warren had come to know as the "you're fucking stupid" smile. "It wouldn't have mattered to her if you had told her a long time ago like I suggested either."

"Yeah, well, hindsight and all that, you know." Warren walked around to the business side of the desk and picked a file he rarely brought out nowadays. "She's gonna be pissed when she finds out what we know."

"Yes, she is. What do you want to do about what may be going down in that little town? If you ask me...." Warren looked at Marshall so that he would finish the statement. "If you were to ask me, I'd say wait. See if she can handle what's going on and see how she comes out on top. You said yourself that you should have put her in charge of the CIA years ago. Now is the perfect opportunity for her to show her stuff and become a national hero at the same time."

"And if she fails? Then what do we show her?" He sat down on the couch again and looked out at the gardens behind the office. "Do we let her fix this, finish this, or do we step in with guns blazing and fix it ourselves?"

"Or," he said softly again, "we could make a trip to the little town and help her out. There's nothing to say that a trip to Ohio would be remiss. Of course, we could get you out of here and no one would be the wiser. We could put you in the hospital for your yearly physical. Might catch a bit of the flu while you're there."

Warren liked the idea. Something was going to go down soon, very soon if what she had told him yesterday was any indication, and he would love to go somewhere and run. He looked out the doors again and thought about running with a pack of cats again. Moving through the woods and….

"Fix it. I think a week should do it. Then another week with the flu." He glanced at the desk. "And while we're there, I want you to help me convince her that she is the perfect man for the job."

The rest of the conversation was said in a normal tone of voice. Neither man mentioned the fact that they were both on their cells making arrangements that would bring Congress down on their heads, not to mention if anyone found out what he really was, maybe even some lab boys. Warren closed his phone an hour later and smiled. He was going to get to do what he'd been dreaming about since he'd taken office three years ago. Run with someone who would not care what he was.

And maybe he wasn't a panther like the Bowens were, but he was a tiger and he knew that once they got to know him as human, then they'd accept him for what he was. A fellow were. At least he hoped so.

~~~

Norris Freeman waited until everyone was off the plane before he stood. He hated people as a rule and less so when they were trapped together like sardines in a tin can at about thirty thousand feet. As he was pulling down his bag from the overhead, the pretty little stewardess came toward him.

"Sir, there's a man outside waiting for you. He asked if you were on board and all we told him was that we couldn't
~~~

release that information. He doesn't look like he's too happy."

Norris thought he probably wasn't.

"Would you like for me to call security and have him escorted out of the airport?"

"No. I'll take care of him."

She nodded, but still looked unsure.

"He isn't a very easy man to make happy. I'll go out and then he'll leave with me. Sorry about this."

Norris didn't think that if the woman were to go out and ask him to leave that he'd walk away. Seth Clarke was not known to be a very forgiving or patient man. His way of doing something was to shoot first and walk away. He'd never known a deadlier man in his life, with the exception of himself, of course. As soon as he stepped off the last step of the walkway he saw why the woman was nervous. He'd be too if he didn't know the man.

"Christ, Clarke, next time why don't you wear a sign that says 'I'm a fucking killer. Stay back if you want to live.' Might draw less attention to yourself." Norris handed him his bag and took the nine millimeter that Seth slipped to him. "What kind of car did you get? If you got one of those small little sporty things I'm fucking going to kill you myself."

"Nah. Got one of those big fucking trucks. Has a nice bed for rolling dead things in and a little holder for all your fancy clothes. Why the fuck would you wear a suit to Ohio? They probably don't even know that that thing cost more than they made all of last year." He ran his finger down the sleeve. "Is that fucking snake?"

"No, you moronic dick, it's silk. And I suppose you are going to make the cover of *GQ* with your torn up jeans and holey shirt? Ever hear of a tailor?"

Clarke laughed, showing that since the last time he'd seen him he'd lost another tooth, this one in the front. "Yeah, I had a Taylor once. But she didn't give good head so I had to fucking shoot her." They went outside and there it was, one of the biggest trucks he'd ever seen. "You wanna drive?"

He didn't bother answering, but got into the passenger side. When they were moving down the highway toward the hotel Clarke turned to him, grinning.

"Ever think we'd get to take out McCray? I mean, holy shit, McCray is the best we've ever seen. I've got a hard-on just thinking about killing her."

Norris looked over at him and grinned too. "You get a hard-on with every kill we do, and ones we don't get to work together on either. But I agree, she is going to be fun. Caitlynne McCray has been a fucking thorn in my side since I shot my first contract."

She'd been at the restaurant where he'd been watching his target for the good part of an hour. He'd paid little attention to her other than to notice that she was beautiful. When he stood up to get the shot, she stood as well and blocked his path. They had smiled at each other, and when she stepped around him, she'd grabbed his arm in what he thought was a small trip. The handcuffs on his wrist were a surprise, as were the nine Federal agents that threw him to the ground and held him down while his target managed to walk out of the busy restaurant. He'd been in jail just long enough for the target to move and he'd had to start all over with tracking him.

It had taken him nearly a year to relocate him and another month to end him. But in the meantime he'd run into McCray three more times until he wanted to bash her skull in just to get her off his trail. Escaping from the small jail had been hard enough, but she seemed to have him in her sights and he hated her for it.

The hotel room was nicer than he'd thought. He'd expected Clarke to have rented the cheapest one he could find in the worst part of town. That way he could still have his fun and have a place to sleep it off afterward.

Clarke killed women. It was his thing. Mostly, if not on a contract, he'd kill only prostitutes, but lately he'd taken to breaking into nicer homes and killing whatever female resided there, leaving the males to wonder what the fuck had happened. He glanced at the man when he sat down in one of the overstuffed chairs.

"You know you have to behave while we do this, right? Garrett said that she is our only target and she needs to be made gone in less than seventy-two hours after we get here."

Clarke smiled and nodded.

"I mean it. I want to be paid for this one, and your habits will not fuck it up for me."

"I know what to do. She dies, it's a free for all. But I get to kill her. She can be dead, but I want the pleasure of killing her." He licked his lips. "I know just how I want to do it too. Slow and easy. I'm going to start by peeling her scalp off. You know how much they scream when you do that?"

Norris turned his back on Clarke when he started rubbing his cock. The man would sit there and jerk off if the mood struck him even if there were a hundred people in the room. When someone knocked on the door, Norris turned back to see that Clarke had his dick out and was jerking off.

"Put that thing away. What the fuck is wrong with you?" Norris went to the door and looked in the peephole. A man was there in a hotel outfit with a large rolling cart in front of him. "Did you order anything?"

"No." Both men pulled out their guns. They stood up with their weapons behind them as Norris opened the door.

The man slid the cart in and smiled at them both. "Here you are, gentlemen. Also, the package that was delivered for you is on the left." He began taking the covers off the food and setting it up on the table near the window. "The gentleman who made the arrangements for this said to tell you it's a lovely day for a ball game. Though I don't believe the season has begun yet. But he said it was important for me to tell you."

Both he and Clarke relaxed. Their contact had sent the dinner and the package. As soon as everything was set up, Clarke sat down at one of the plates and the waiter moved toward the door. Norris pulled out his wallet to tip the man and he told him he'd been taken care of. He left before Norris sat.

They both ate in silence. The dinner was what both would have ordered. Steak for Clarke and a nice piece of salmon for him. The salad was perfect, as was the wine for him and a cold draft for Clarke. They both finished their meal before opening the package.

It was everything they had on her and then some. Her address, the type of vehicle she drove, and the kind of gun she preferred. It seemed to Norris that she liked them all, including any kind of knife. He handed the one picture they had been given of her to Clarke. She was still as beautiful as ever.

"Damn, you didn't tell me that she was a redhead. All you said was she was a pretty little thing." Clarke handed it back. "How tall is she anyway?"

He thought she was around six foot, but wasn't sure. He told Clarke that she was still off limits until they had a plan. The girl was lethal and there wasn't any joking about that.

Clarke snorted, something that Norris had always hated about him.

"She can't be all that hard to take. I mean, she is only a woman."

Norris rolled his eyes, but before he could comment, Clarke continued.

"Why don't you let me go and bring her back and you can have some fun with her before I get her? You'd better rest up too, 'cause I got a feeling she's a wildcat in bed."

Norris thought about letting him go and do just that, but told him to stay put. According to the information they'd been sent, she was staying at a doctor's house and there was little to no security around the place. He told Clarke that they'd go and get her tomorrow night after getting some sleep. He'd come in from across the world and he thought that Clarke had been down under. They both went to their separate bedrooms in the suite. Norris took a long, hot shower.

Tomorrow, he'd have the bitch. And when he did he'd make her pay for every moment he had doubted himself after the restaurant debacle. It had taken nearly five years to get another well-paying job and two more before he felt like he was the man he'd been. And all because some cunt had decided to stand up and have him arrested when he'd been there first.

Norris went to the door to listen for Clarke. When he didn't hear anything, he went to the bedroom door and looked in. The man was already in bed and the room was silent. Norris went back to his room, closed the door, and crawled into bed as well. He closed his eyes, smiling about the fun they were going to have with the bitch in less than twenty-four hours.

CHAPTER THIRTEEN

Lynne went from sleeping to across the room in seconds. She had no idea what had startled her awake, but she wasn't going to take a chance by laying there waiting for it to take her. The low voice from across the room where she'd been made her tense up tighter.

"What are you doing up in the middle of the night? Come back to bed and let me sleep for another couple of hours before you jump around like that." She didn't move. "Caitlynne?"

"Why do you call me that?" She had no idea where that question came from, but now that she thought about it, she wanted answers. "No one else in the world calls me that and you insist on doing it. Why can't you just call me Lynne or McCray?"

She heard him move around on the bed and wondered why it sounded so loud. "Because it's your name and I happen to love it. And I refuse to call you McCray. That sounds like we're in a locker room full of football players. Come back to bed."

She didn't move. There was something wrong and she couldn't quite put her finger on it. When he moved again she thought it sounded like he was right next to her. She flinched at the sound. Before she could comment, he spoke.

"You're feeling some major effects right now, and if you come back to bed, I'll explain what I can. Are you sore?"

She tried to think why she'd be sore when she remembered the bite he'd given her. She put her hand over her neck and shook her head, forgetting he couldn't see her. "No. I don't hurt. I feel weird, but I'm not hurt." She did feel off. Not really a bad kind of off, but not her usual self either. "What happened after we had sex?" She knew he had stood up, and when he walked toward her she could see him in the dark room. When he was standing close to her she thought she could hear his heart beating too. Lynne looked up into his eyes and realized she could see them as if it were bright in the room. "Walker, what's going on?" He picked her up, something he had been doing a lot, and sat with her in a chair. She was suddenly afraid, and she never got afraid.

"Don't freak out on me. And please let me finish before you draw your gun."

She got up off his lap and sat in the opposite chair. She reached for her gun on the table and held it. "Talk." He leaned back in the chair and stared at her. She felt the hair on her arms and neck tingle. She looked at the door when someone walked in. It was Khan. He looked pissed.

"You're a part of this family now, and I'm here for you to pledge yourself to me."

She looked over at Walker and back at Khan. He seemed to be serious. "Fuck off, buddy. I didn't swear to the president; I'm not going to do you either." Walker laughed, and she decided that shooting him was too easy. He was going to die by bleeding to death as she pulled his hairs out one follicle at a time.

"I told you this was a waste of time. Why you changed her is beyond me."

Khan stomped out of the room, and she looked at Walker. Changed her? "If you don't explain to me what the fuck that meant, I will shoot you on principle."

He grinned at her.

"I mean it, talk to me."

"I accidentally converted you."

She looked around the room and back at him.

"You're now like me…well, like us."

"I'm assuming you don't mean you've converted me to some religious cult or something." He shook his head. "Converted me to what?"

"Panther. When I bit you and you me it started the change in you. It wasn't something I planned, and I certainly hadn't meant for it to happen, but my cat took over, and when you—" She raised her hand, and he stopped talking.

She put the gun on the table, not sure she wouldn't use it on him right now and she wanted answers. Pacing helped, but didn't get her any closer to understanding what he was talking about. "Explain to me what exactly that means for me being a panther." She stopped him again when he took a deep breath. "In quick, easy terms. I don't think I can handle a long, drawn-out explanation right now."

"I let my cat bite you for him to mark you. You bit me too. During the exchange, he tore at you and made a deeper wound than he should have. His essence filled you and he changed you. We changed you."

"He's not a part of you?"

He nodded his head, and she frowned.

"Then how is it that he changed me and not you? You blaming him for something that you did?"

"No. I didn't mean it.... I wanted you to be converted, but didn't want to take the chance that you'd die. Only about one or two percent of humans can handle it. It's painful and a long process. Most humans die within hours of the initial bite."

"But I didn't." When he shook his head, she paced some more. "Can I change into a panther?"

"I don't know. Like I said, very few humans live—"

"Could you please stop calling us humans? I'm a little overwhelmed right now, and I'm trying my best not to kill you. Call it...I don't know, call us people."

"But you're not human any longer."

That stopped her in her tracks. She turned to look at him and he shrugged.

"And you can't hurt me either. Not now. It'll be in your DNA."

"That you know, but you haven't a clue if I can change." She picked up the gun and pointed it at him. He was right. She couldn't do it. Tossing it back on the dresser, she stalked around the room again. "So your cat changed me into something you don't know about, and you have no clue what I can do, and aren't even sure that in a few hours I might not keel over and die. Just great. Anything else you've neglected to tell me?" He grinned at her, and she glared back. "What?"

"The president is downstairs in our living room. And he's not human either."

She sat down hard. It might not have hurt so badly if there had been a chair or even the bed behind her, but she hit the floor.

"What is he?" She spoke softly, but knew that he could hear her. "What is he if not human? A panther?"

"Weretiger. And his aide is too. Mr. David is a yellow Bengal, and the president is a white Bengal. They both have come to help and run on the property." Walker stood up and moved toward her slowly. "They want to talk to you. They've been waiting for over an hour."

She didn't reach for his hand, but stared at it. He hunkered down to look her in the eye, and she felt a connection. It snapped into place like a rubber band to the wrist.

"You and I are a mated couple. We'll be able to speak like this over long distances no matter where you are. Try and talk to me with your mind, love."

She shook her head.

"You have to try. You might need me, or I you, and if it doesn't work both ways we won't be able to help one another."

"I'm a little...okay, I'm fucking overwhelmed right now. Not about the changing stuff, though I'm still having issues with that one, but the president? And Marshall?" She looked toward the door where Khan had gone. *"And he wants me to pledge myself to him? Why? So he can pretend to protect me? I'm not sure he'd do that even if I pledged to have his baby."*

His growl made her smile. *"According to law, anyone new to the family has to make sure they are pledged to us. That way we can hear each other's thoughts. Not the ones you and I have, but when we're a group."* She started to ask him if they were a pack when he answered it for her. *"Panthers are called groups, not packs. Wolves run in packs, not us. There are different names for each of the species of cat. We're simply called a group or, with us, a family."*

She let him pull her up off the floor and they moved toward the door. "Will Warren be able to hear us speaking? I mean as a group?"

"No. He's something entirely different than us. He will be able to hear other tigers so long as they're Bengals."

They hit the last stair and she turned to him. "You have to trust me."

He nodded.

"I mean it. No matter what, you have to trust me that I know what I'm doing. I'm trained in this. Promise me."

He kissed her and then nodded again. "I promise to trust you in all things that you do concerning your work and job. But the rest…we'll have to work on that one. Is that enough?"

It was and she told him so. Pulling away from him, she entered the large living room and accounted for everyone in the room. The only person who wasn't present was Khan, but she didn't really care at the moment.

~~~

Warren stood when she entered. She was as beautiful as ever. Before he could tell her how happy he was to see her, she stopped, turned slightly, and came around in a roundhouse punch that took him to the floor and a few feet away. Marshall stood up and, before he could move, she had a gun plastered to his forehead.

"Move and I will blow what little brains you have in that thick skull of yours all over the nice books behind you."

He wasn't sure if she was talking to him or Marshall, but neither of them moved.

"Now, we're going to have a little talk about truth and lies. Like the one you told me before I started working for you when Melvin was murdered."

"I never actually lied to you, Lynne. I simply didn't disclose everything." She pulled out a second gun and pointed at him as he continued. "Okay, maybe that was lying to you, but I didn't want you to be…."

"Be what? Afraid? Turn away from you? You moron, you should have told me. You should have trusted me as I did you." She glanced to her right when one of the people on the
~~~

couch moved. "He'll be dead before you get to me. Sit down."

Warren looked over at the young man he'd been introduced to as Reed. The boy looked pissed, and he didn't blame him, but Warren knew that she would shoot him if someone interceded on his part. She was very hot tempered when she wanted to be. "Lynne, this is getting us no closer to getting this family safe. Can't we just sit down and talk this over? I swear to you that I will never lie to you, neither by omission nor by lies." She looked at Marshall who looked ready to attack her. He reached out for the man and begged him not to let her kill him. The quick glance his way made him think that Marshall was going to make him pay for this.

"Right now, we're on a short fuse. You fuck me over and I will murder you both. I'm fucking sick of all this bullshit, and you both are well aware of what I've done to keep you both safe." He nodded and stood up. Marshall didn't move when she took the gun off him, and when she put out her hand to him, he was sure the man wasn't going to take it.

"I'm pissed at you."

She nodded at Marshall's bald statement.

"You could have hurt him. Hurting him is not an option."

"I'm well aware of what I did. And I'm well aware of the consequences of my actions." She stepped closer to him and lowered her voice. "I'm not your average agent."

Walker burst out laughing. Warren hadn't realized that the man hadn't moved when she was handling them. He looked back at Lynne, then the young man. They were a couple. But he decided that congratulating them now might still get him shot. Before anyone could sit down and begin again, a cell phone sounded and Mrs. Bowen answered. He knew immediately that something was wrong.

She paled and looked at Lynne. Before the elderly woman could stand, Lynne was kneeling in front of her, taking the phone. She looked over at him and nodded. Christ, it was bad when she looked like that.

He watched her move. She was water in motion when she was working, and he put his hand in front of Marshall when he looked to be going to help her. Her end of the conversation was full of humor, smart-assed replies. It was what she was doing that had him wishing he had a camera to show others what a real agent was supposed to do.

The laptop was on the small table in front of her. She continued speaking and hooking the phone up to it. When the cursor started zooming across the screen and clicking on icons he had no idea what she was doing. When Reed leaned over to him, the man explained.

"She's tracking the number. He doesn't think she can because it's not her phone. She showed us that gizmo a couple of days ago. She said that she can track a phone on that program that most big leaguers can't." He listened to her for a few seconds before grinning. "She does have a colorful way of putting things, doesn't she?"

Warren nodded. He wasn't altogether sure about some of the names she was calling the person on the other end, but he was reasonably sure it was keeping him on the line to insult her back. It seemed to be working, and when the computer beeped once and pulled up a map, Warren watched as it flashed up an address. She had him.

When she handed the phone back to Mrs. Bowen, she held her hand. "I will get him back for you. I swear to you I will.

"Get who back from whom? And if you think you're leaving this house without me, then you can rethink that right fucking now." Walker reached for her and pulled her into his arms. "Tell me. Tell me what's going on before I have a shit fit."

"They have Khan. They don't know who he is; well, that's not true. They think he's you. They think they have my lover and that I will come along nicely to save him." She glanced over at him as she continued. "Do you remember Seth Clarke and Norris Freeman?"

"Yes. They've been on the FBI's most wanted for nearly ten years. Christ, they don't have him, do they?" She nodded, and he had to sit down. He had to think. Those two men were lethal when apart; together, they were a nightmare.

"I'll get him. They don't know it yet, but they're both dead." She pointed to the computer screen. "They are working with Small."

He shook his head. "Can't be. I had him tossed just yesterday. There isn't any way for him to contact anyone now. I even had him moved to another cell. There's no way he could have contacted them." She smiled, and he knew he had missed something.

"As standard policy, you had him moved to the next cell. Right next to the one he had before so he can see what he no longer has."

He nodded slowly.

"He had it planted there. That's what I would have done. And for the record, they said that Garrett contacted them. But they said they'd been in contact with someone that would make you disappear soon enough. Only one with a hard-on to do that would be Small."

"Mother fuck."

He couldn't have agreed more with Marshall.

"Now what do we do? What's the plan?"

"My plan is to go in and get Khan and bring him back here." Warren started to speak, but she stopped him with her raised hand. "You can't go in, and you know why. If you're hurt, how will you explain to anyone why you were here?"

"You'll need backup. Who can I trust to help you?" Warren wasn't surprised to see Walker raise his hand. But the others, including the older couple doing so, did. He looked over at Marshall who had as well.

"See, instant backup." Lynne looked at Mr. and Mrs. Bowen. "You two need to stay here. And before you argue, let me explain. I'll need someone to come and get anyone who's hurt and bring them back. I'm guessing that, once this hits the fan, there will be people all over this. Someone needs to carry out the wounded."

"You think that's going to happen?" Walker looked terrified and Warren didn't blame the man. "You think that someone is going to get killed?"

"Not if I can help it." She looked at Marshall. "I need you to give me an hour before you call in the troops. You'll need to take care of Small too. His cell will need to be put into lockdown and the service cut off, or he needs to be put into another place."

"Consider it done." He smiled at her. "You're a scary bitch when you want to be, aren't you?"

She nodded, sat down on the floor near the computer, and started barking orders to the five men standing around her. Before she left thirty minutes later, the plan was set. Warren looked at the remaining people and smiled.

"She'll do it too. You have to have faith that she'll do everything that she said she'll do and then some. I'd trust her with my life."

Mr. Bowen snorted. "We trusted her with all six of our lives. And we believe in her very much."

CHAPTER FOURTEEN

The plan was set, and she wasn't tense like she normally was before a mission. She looked over at the group of men who she supposed were now her family. She took Walker's hand and held it while she spoke to them all.

"When I go in, you'll all need to stay back. I won't be able to make sure that you aren't killed while trying to save Khan. He's not going to cooperate as it is, and I don't want to have to try to save more than one furry ass at a time." Reed laughed, as did the others. "Also, I need to show you something in my truck."

They all went out to her vehicle that had been parked in the garage since she'd been here. Backing it out of the parking place, she showed each of them the small mechanism under the steering column that would release the explosive that she had on the engine.

"Anyone who gets in and tries to start it without turning this will be killed. The truck is wired to some pretty high octane stuff, and there won't be a baggie's worth of stuff left to find." Each of them took a step back. She didn't want to scare them, but she didn't want them hurt either. "Also, there's something else you should know." She motioned for

Reed to come forward and stand next to the truck. She knew he was curious about the weight of it. She took his hand and put it under the seat just to the left of the middle of it. "Feel those?" He nodded. "They're coded to be pushed in a certain order. If you don't, then you don't get what's inside."

He grinned. "A woman that's as beautiful as you? Or do we get all the cash you have stashed under the seat? I bet you get paid well to be what you are."

"I do, but that's all in the bank in a nice safety deposit box. There are three buttons. Push them in this order. Number two, number one, then number two twice. Don't fuck up." He grinned at her and asked her why. "Because if you do, then it will cut off your dick and you bleed to death."

He jerked his hand out so quickly that he nearly knocked them both over. The rest of them cupped themselves as if she wasn't kidding them. Taking his hand again, she put it back under the seat and told him to press the buttons.

"I was kidding, you idiot. Press the fucking buttons. You'll each have to do this to make sure you can before you need to." He pressed the buttons when she told him to and stepped back. "Okay, this is not to be played around with. And when this shit is over, I'm going to make sure all of you can shoot, and shoot well. Understand?" When they nodded, she lifted the seat up. It had cost her a great deal of money to have this truck outfitted. She had wanted something that she could save herself with if necessary, and anyone else if it came to that. She'd only had to use it once before and had decided that no matter the cost, she'd not eat for a year before she'd not have this little treasure chest where she could get it.

The seat lifted, and on the bottom of it were three rifles, each of them loaded with ammo as well as scopes. There were two handguns, both Glocks, as well as a flashlight and a first aid kit. The bottom of the seat, the part that was supposed to be the cushion, was filled as well. There was a small carrying case that was filled with fifty thousand dollars and two passports, neither of them hers. There were also some credit cards, a few driver's licenses, as well as a couple of birth certificates. Again, not hers.

In addition to that, there were nine boxes of shells for the rifles and eight boxes of ammo for the Glocks. She watched as they each took a turn looking at her stash, and then one of them asked if there was anything going to blow if they got this far and needed to take something out.

"No. Once you get it opened, the stuff is there for the taking. Leave the bag, though. There's nothing in there that would help you, and I will hunt you down if you do." All of them nodded, and she was glad she'd not cracked a smile. She'd been only bluffing, but she wanted them to have their game faces on for tonight.

The rest of the equipment was just as lethal. There were two more rifles, these sniper style, as well as a couple of handguns that she had loved and couldn't part with once she'd used them. An assortment of knives, honed to a sharp edge, were there, as well as a couple of things she was sure would get her arrested if found. The small explosives were enough to take out a large building and maybe a city block if she set them correctly. Which she would. Ammo enough to fight off a small army, as well as two cell phones that were off but fully charged, and some dehydrated food packages that if she got to a point where she was in a standoff situation, she could survive. There was a case of bottled water as well.

Each man took their turn in opening the seat. They stood marveling at the stuff a great deal longer than necessary, but when she started to tell them they needed to finish the plan, Walker took her away from the truck and toward a tree a few feet away. His mouth covered hers before she could ask him what he was doing.

He was hard against her and she found herself wanting him to take her right then and there. When she ran her fingers down his chest and to his cock, he rocked into her hand twice before he lifted his head.

"I think we've planned enough for now. I want to take you upstairs and make love to you before I can think about anything else." He licked along her throat, then nipped at her. "Tell me you want me too. Tell me that I can send them on their way and take you."

"Yes. Tell them. But take me here. I want to feel you inside of me out here." The men laughed, and she started to turn toward them when they shouted they were leaving. She looked at him with a raised brow.

"I can talk to them through our family connection. You will be able to once you and Khan get things settled between you. If you don't, then so what? I can translate." He tore her shirt open then lifted her bra up and over her breasts. "So warm. I love the way you taste."

He suckled her nipple hard and she tangled her fingers into his hair. Christ, he was going to make her come just like this. When he pinched the other nipple, she moaned and held him to her. She came, screaming out his name.

~~~

Walker dropped to his knees in front of her and ripped her pants off. He couldn't wait any longer to drink from her. Burying his mouth between her thighs, he suckled her clit into his mouth and entered her with his fingers. Her second climax was delicious and hot. He drank greedily of her until she was begging him to stop.

"No, I can't. I want you to come again. You've no idea how much I love the taste of you. Come for me, baby. Come
~~~

in my mouth again, then I'll lean you over that tree and fuck you until you can't walk."

She nodded at him and he flicked his tongue over her nub. She was ready that quickly, but he wanted to enjoy her a little more. Spreading her thighs, he lifted her right leg, positioned it over his shoulder, and ate at her, suckled on her nether lips until she was dancing her hips closer to him. Every time she got close, nearly falling over the edge, he would back off. Twice he lifted his head and watched her as she gathered herself.

"Walker, if you don't finish me I'm going to go over to my truck and shoot your dick off with one of my guns. I'm serious. I need to come."

He did as well. Standing up, he led her to the truck and had her lean over it. Coming up behind her, he unsnapped his pants and released his aching cock. She turned to look at him and licked her lips. He decided that if she wanted to take him, who was he to deny her?

She dropped down much like he had and immediately took his cock deep into her throat. He had to grab onto the hood of the truck or fall over. She didn't give him any kind of lead up, but had him deep before he could catch his breath. When she cupped his balls, he grabbed her head and held her while he fucked her. He loved feeling his cock touch the back of her throat, and when she swallowed, he cried out her name.

Lifting her up, he turned her around so her ass was toward him. He knew she was ready; he could smell her. Slamming deeply into her, he leaned over her and licked along her spine. She was sweaty and sweet and he wanted more. Reaching around to her pussy, he slid his finger inside of her and could feel his cock every time. When she started to push back, he pinched her clit hard and sank his teeth deep into her shoulder. His own release made his eyes roll in the back of his head.

Neither of them moved for several minutes. He wasn't sure if he'd ever be able to, but when she giggled he lifted his head off her, and the wound he'd inflicted on her closed. She sighed when he kissed her.

"Your brothers know what we're about?"

He thought they probably did since he'd told them to get the fuck away from there.

"I'm sure you weren't very nice when you got rid of them."

"I wasn't. When they get their own mates they'll know what I mean." He looked around the empty yard for their clothes. "I'm afraid you'll have to go inside naked. I seem to have lost myself with your smell."

Caitlynne turned to look at him. The change had made her eyes bluer and her skin softer. He ran his finger over her throat and watched her face. She smiled at him. "I don't know how I lived all this time without you." She nodded at him as he continued. "I never really cared if I found a mate, didn't really understand how much they could make a change in my life. But I've fallen in love with you. I can't…tonight, you have to be extra careful and come back to me."

"I will. I swear it." She kissed his chin, leaned back against the truck, and stared at him. "Walker, there's something you should know. Something that will be important to you if I don't make it ou—"

"No. I don't want to think like that. Please, not right now. I just want to hold you like this until we have to go inside and get ready. Please?" She nodded and then laid her head on his chest. "I love you, Caitlynne."

"I love you too. I don't…I don't want to cause a problem for you and your family, but Khan really hates me." He nodded. "I have a house closer to DC that I can live in, and you can come and visit me sometimes."

He lifted her head and looked down at her. "Wherever you go, we go. I won't spend another day without you. If this thing between you two doesn't work out, I can get a job anywhere. I'm a very good doctor. Don't worry about it now. We'll get him out, and he'll be so grateful that he'll drop to his knees and kiss your feet."

She laughed, and he decided that it was the most wondrous sound he'd ever heard. He couldn't wait to have children with her…small little girls that looked just like her and acted…well, maybe not acted just like her, but close. He could see them running in the yard and playing. Maybe even a son or two. Before he could voice his needs, her phone rang somewhere behind them.

By the time they found it, the person had left a voicemail. The second time it started to ring, she answered. He watched the change on her face and knew it was the people who had Khan. She told them she'd meet them somewhere in two hours. They both ran to the house as she hung up.

"They want me to meet them about four miles or so, I'd guess, from where they called me from the first time. The caller said that they'd have him there for the exchange." She pulled on panties and a bra.

"You don't think he'll be there, I take it."

She shook her head and pulled on dark pants and a darker shirt.

"Where are you planning to go?"

She grinned. It wasn't terribly friendly; neither did it reach her eyes. If she turned that on him for whatever reason other than to show him she was pissed at someone else, he knew right then and there that whatever she wanted, it was hers.

"Why, I go where your brother is. You'll need to tell me how to make that mind thingy your mom was talking about work."

It took him several seconds to try to work out what she meant and remembered hearing his mom tell her about some of the things she could do as a panther. "You didn't pledge to him. You have no connection to him, so it won't work." She sat down and pulled on her boots. "But it will with us. I can relay whatever you need. He'd probably do the opposite of what you wanted anyway."

She nodded, but looked concerned. "What makes you think he won't do that anyway? I mean, if he doesn't listen to either of us, he will get us both killed. And I don't know about you, but I'm not in the mood to die at the moment."

She was joking, he knew that, but the reality of what was going to happen hit him hard, right in his heart. He walked to her, pulled her up, and held her to him. He wasn't in the mood to let her die either and told her so.

"He'll be stubborn, Walker. He won't listen, and he'll try to do things his way. Please make him understand that I know what I'm doing. He has to trust me."

Walker knew she was right. Right about Khan not listening to them, and also that he had to trust her. But he wouldn't. And Walker was terrified that Khan would get them both hurt.

"I'll tell him. I'll even threaten him. But you have to be ready for that, all right? You have to be ready for him to be the Khan we all know and love." She laughed and pulled away. "I know, you have to get going. But tell me again that you love me."

"I love you. Now get dressed, we have to go."

He drove this time and loved the way her truck handled. When she turned off the radio he glanced over at her. She had her phone out and was tapping on the screen. Suddenly, the cab of the truck was filled with voices.

"Okay. I want team one to be at the place where I'm supposed to go, and team two at the warehouse." She winked at him. "Walker and I are on our way to your parents' house to tell them what we know. Are there any questions?"

The phone was on speaker, and he could hear his brothers laughing and making several suggestions on what they wanted to do to the men they were going after. They were nervous; he could hear it in their tones and the way they didn't seem to want to take this seriously. But he knew that they would once it was go time.

The meeting with his parents was short. They needed to get going and they both seemed to know it. When his dad hugged Caitlynne, she hugged him back and Walker realized that his cat didn't seem to mind. When he purred along his skin, Walker wrapped his arms around both his parents as well as Caitlynne and knew that both he and his cat needed this.

"Bring him back to me, dear. I want him here so I can kick his bottom for getting caught so we had to do this."

Caitlynne nodded.

"And you had better come back to us as well. I want to see grandchildren. We want to bounce them on our knees before we're too old to enjoy it."

"I will. I'll make sure that he comes back to you whole and his usual sarcastic self." Caitlynne gave a short bark of laughter. "Maybe he might like me after this. Who knows?"

When they were about a mile from the warehouse they parked the truck. She opened the seat up, handed him a Glock, and took out two for herself. She helped him out by showing him how to keep it on him and not get a track cut when he had to use it.

"When this is done I'm going to make sure all of you know how to use a gun. You may not ever need it again, I hope not anyway, but if we stick around here, I don't want them to freak out when I come in the house armed." He nodded. "I don't want to have to quit my job, Walker. I'm really good at it and I love it."

"Why would you even think that I'd want you to? You are good at this, and I'm reasonably sure that someone is going to have to run the program now that Garrett is gone." Walker wanted her home, fat with child, but he didn't know what he'd do if someone told him he couldn't be a doctor. "You get my brother out safely, and you as well. We'll talk about places to live, jobs, and other things later."

"And kids? Do you want them too? We never talked about that."

He kissed her instead of answering her and she turned to the building. "Go. Go and finish this. I have a desire to take you to bed again and make love to you all night."

She turned to walk toward the building, but came back. Her mouth covered his, and he pressed her against the truck. He loved this woman and didn't know what he'd do without her if something went wrong in there.

CHAPTER FIFTEEN

Khan woke, but kept his head down. He hurt in more places than he thought there were names for. Listening to the sounds around him, he realized that he wasn't alone. There were at least two humans with him. He tried to judge just how far they were from him, and he couldn't with all the other sounds going on in the room.

He thought they were in a large warehouse. And from the sounds and smells, he'd say it had been closed for some time. He could smell dirt and neglect, and the two men with him had a scent of death and sex. He tried to focus on what they were saying, but he hurt too badly. Letting his body go, he slipped away from them and deep into his cat to let him heal too.

The next time he woke he knew that at least one of the men had left the area. Khan could smell burgers and greasy fries on top of the odor of something more...beer or something close to it. He felt his belly rebel at the smells and tried to take deep breaths in his nose so as not to be sick. But he had figured out one thing; the man was in front of him, about ten feet away.

Khan took an inventory of his injuries. He wasn't hurting nearly as badly as the first time he'd awakened, but he was still hurt. He could see the white plastic strips around his wrists, and when he tried to move his feet, he could feel them biting into his flesh there as well. With them being so tight around his wrists and ankles he couldn't shift. If he did and they didn't break, he would sever one, if not all, of his appendages.

He raised his head slowly when he heard a soft snore. The man was sleeping in a chair with his head resting on the table in front of him. There were several fast food bags in front of him. Some of his food had hit the floor and two rats were grabbing up what they could. Khan quietly snarled his cat at them and they took off quickly. If only he could do the same for the man.

A window to his right showed him it was twilight out. He reached for one of his brothers, but the pain in his head was too great and he had to stop. Looking around the rest of the room, he saw a door as well as a large garage door. He had an idea where he might be, but without seeing the outside of the building, he couldn't be sure. When the door opened he dropped his head again and listened while the newcomer yelled at the other man for sleeping.

"What the fuck does it matter? He's still out. I told you not to hit him that hard, that we should have just shot him to bring him down." The laughter of the two men had his skin crawl. "He sure is a big one. I'd hate to fuck with him man to man. He's probably fucking McCray hard, don't you think?"

He didn't much care for them talking about his brother's mate that way. He didn't like her either, but no one messed with his family. He started to raise his head when he smelled cat. Panther.

The door opened with a bang and there she stood, as if brought to life simply by talking about her. Khan didn't want to be impressed by her, but she looked like she could kick ass and still want to know where to go for dinner. She looked over at him and winked. He nearly looked behind him to see who she was looking at.

"Hello, honey. Are you all right?"

Khan nodded, not sure what else to do when she asked.

"Good. These nice men are going to let you go and then we—"

"I don't think so. You stay away from him."

Khan hadn't realized that she'd been moving toward him until the fatter man had stopped her.

"And he isn't going anywhere until you're right where we want you."

At first, Khan tried to ignore the touch of his mind. He was too busy trying to figure out how to save the dumbass woman in front of him and get them both out alive. When he realized it was Walker, he snarled at him to leave him the fuck alone.

"She's trying to help you, you jackass. Now listen to me."

Khan told his brother she was going to get them killed when Walker laughed.

"Not likely. She wants to know if you have anything wrapped around your ankles or feet. She can't see them."

"Plastic strips like at my wrists. I can't shift." He waited for Walker to say something like he was coming to get him when he spoke again.

"She said when she comes toward you not to snarl at her, but to act like you're me. Those men think that they have her lover, and they told her that they're going to trade you for her."

"She's not thinking she can take these two on, is she? She doesn't even have a gun on her, and they have...." He counted. *"They have five guns on them that I can see."*

"You may not like her, but she's the only hope you have of coming out alive. And when she helps you, she said not to move until she tells you to. She said to tell you that she doesn't have time to make sure you're not killed while she's taking care of the bad guys." Walker laughed. *"Actually, she said humans, but I didn't want to piss you off."*

He was pissed. Pissed to think that she of all people thought she could save him. When she started toward him again, he saw her body move and knew that she wasn't armed at all. She leaned to him and her mouth was a breath away. "Don't move." Her hand moved along his wrist and he felt the pressure of the plastic let go. Then she slipped something into his freed hand. When she moved her mouth close to his, she whispered again. "For you."

The kiss was brief and he felt her slip something into his mouth. He didn't know what it was, but it had a metallic taste. Khan put it in his cheek and waited. When she stopped in front of him, he looked down at the small knife under his hand.

She'd cut his tie and had given him a way of getting free. When she didn't move but continued to talk to the idiots in front of them, he reached over and cut the other strip. He wasn't sure how to cut the ones at his ankles when she moved from in front of him.

"Caitlynne said to tell you not to move. She said if you do, you could get both of you killed." His brother sounded terrified. He didn't blame him; so was he.

"Where are you and when are you coming in to save us? She can't possibly think that she can do this on her own."

Walker laughed. *"She does and she will. We're close, but not inside the building. She doesn't know how to tell if someone is human or not. I can't tell from here."*

Khan felt the hair on his arms dance and his cat snarl at him when the men aimed their guns at her. *"They're going to kill her. I have to do something."*

"No." His brother wasn't there; he couldn't see the danger she was in. *"Khan, you'll get her killed."*

He watched them speaking and reached down and cut the strips from his ankles. When they were cut, he put his hands back on the armrests and waited. When Lynne turned to look at him, one of the men raised their weapons and pointed it at her. Khan moved just as she did.

Khan hit the floor when Lynne's body slammed against his. He looked at the two men and saw that one was leaning against the wall with blood trickling from his forehead and the other man was lying down as well. Neither of them moved when he dumped Lynne off him.

"What the fuck were you doing? I told you to stay still."

He walked over to the two men and checked their pulse as Lynne continued to berate him.

"You fucking bastard, you were told I had this under control."

He turned to look at her and saw she had been shot. "Christ. What the hell happened?"

"What the fuck does it look liked happened? I had to move so you wouldn't get your dumb ass killed. You couldn't die." He looked at the two dead men and back at her as she loaded another clip into her gun. "They were going to kill you when you moved and I promised your mom I'd bring you back."

The blood was pouring from her chest…her abdomen too. She'd leapt in front of him, he remembered, and not behind him like he'd screamed at her to do. The one in her chest would have caught him in the heart had she not—

"Look at me, Lynne. You need to pledge to me. Right now, you need to pledge to me." He jerked her face to his when she closed her eyes. He could hear her heart slowing. She was losing blood fast.

"Now? I don't think so. I'm tired. Tell Walker I'm sorry." She was sounding far away and he was afraid for her.

"Pledge to me. Now." She looked at him, her eyes fading. He could hear her breaths slowing. "Please, Lynne, now, or I can't bring your cat to save you."

"You can't save me, dickhead. Why would you want to?"

He looked up when four cats entered the room, one of them a large white Bengal. Khan looked down at her as Walker came toward them as a human with a medical bag in his hand. Khan was terrified it was too late for anything he might have in that bag.

Her voice was low, but he heard it. With those two little words, he commanded her cat to come forth. It was a horrible and extremely painful way to shift, but she would have a chance if she shifted. When her cat began to appear he watched her still. He just hoped he wasn't too late.

~~~

Warren looked at the man sitting chained to the table. He wasn't much of a man, short and thin, but he had a wealth of information. He glanced down at the yellow pad that he'd been taking notes on, then back at the man.

"You said that Small is working for someone in Afghanistan? Do you know who?"

Nestor nodded and grinned. "He's a captain in the United States Marine Corps. His name is Jackson. I don't know if I ever heard his first name, but I know what he looks like. He calls too. Would you like his cell phone number?"
~~~

Numbly, he pushed the pad at him again and watched as he wrote this number down too. There were a total of ten names on the first sheet alone, as well as last known address and phone numbers. Warren nodded at Marshall. He would take the name they'd just been given and search for him in their database. He glanced at Reed Bowen, who was helping them with the searches.

"They've been working together for nearly ten years, well before he decided to be in politics. But Jackson insisted that they could make more money if there was someone on the inside that could get the information to them firsthand." Nestor laughed. "They were cutting out the middle man, you see."

"And how did you get involved?" Reed had done that three times now, asking questions without consulting anyone first. But instead of telling him to shut up and do his job like he'd been asked to do, Warren was beginning to like where the kid's head was.

"Oh that was easy. I was in the right place at the right time, you might say. I knew that he'd wanted his family killed and had helped him get them all together. He said that they knew things about him that, if questioned, he wouldn't be able to have a library card much less run for any kind of office. I knew things as well, but I told him that they were somewhere safe and that if he didn't take me along, or something unknown happened to me, then I'd make sure he was buried right along with me. It's sometimes nice to have a little dirt on the person you're working for. It makes things so much easier when you have to tell them no."

Warren didn't have a clue what he was talking about, but nodded all the same.

He looked down at the file Marshall had gone to get when Nestor had been arrested trying to leave the country. Nestor had sang like a bird as soon as he'd been approached, starting with telling Marshall that he had enough evidence on Small that what Caitlynne had would look like child's play. Warren was beginning to believe him. He'd told them where to find this information as well as a whole lot of other things.

"Jeffery Jackson, last known address is in Washington. He has a house in Florida and one in France. He has eight thousand dollars in his bank account and the last deposit was just over two weeks ago for seven hundred twelve dollars and four cents." Reed glanced at him then at Nestor. "Do you know if he has an offshore account?"

"Oh my, yes. We all do. I don't have Jackson's number, but I do have the information on mine and Jerry's." He didn't even ask this time, but took the pad back and wrote down all the information on both accounts. "I'm also putting the account information on two other accounts you may want to look into. One of them is Conrad's, God rest his soul, and the other belongs to Norris Freeman. I don't believe you have him in custody as of yet."

"No. No we don't." Warren slid the information over to Reed and watched him tap on the keys of his laptop for several seconds before he looked at Nestor again. "What is his involvement in all of this? I mean, his name has never come up be—"

Marshall cleared his throat before speaking. "He's on the FBI's most wanted. He's attached to several murders of key people all over the world. He's been known to work with a partner on occasion, but who—"

"Oh, that would be Seth Clarke. He's a terrible man and I've no use for him, but he did seem to get the job done." Nestor looked at Reed. "You may want to see if there are any unsolved murders of prostitutes in the area lately. If they are blond and tall, that would be his work. He had a fetish for murdering them, then having sex with them. As I said, a terrible man."

Reed looked at him for the first time. He could see the horror in his eyes and waited for him to bolt. He was just a kid, probably only in his early to mid-twenties, but he seemed to know his computer stuff. When he looked back at Nestor he thought the boy was going to tell him he was lying or, at the very least, tell him that he was wrong about him being only terrible.

"If you could give me some time frames that he's been in the city, I could see what I could find. Or if you know them, giving me some places he might have been might help a few precincts solve some of their murders. I believe that would help the president too when this goes to trial."

Warren decided that as soon as this was over he was going to see if this kid would come and work for him. He had a good head on his shoulders, as well as a talent not to lose his cool when things looked bad. He looked over at Marshall when his phone rang. While Nestor told Reed dates and places that he knew where Clarke had been, Warren thought about all the information they had to take Small down.

Marshall didn't look happy when he shut off his phone. "There's been an accident. They got Khan out, but our operative has been…hurt."

"How bad?"

Marshall shook his head.

"Can you take over here? I have to get to them. She has to live."

"If you mean Caitlynne McCray, I wouldn't worry about her living. As soon as Jerry is president she's as good as dead anyway." Nestor smiled at them. "He has never liked her, and when she told him she was going to personally see him standing before a firing squad and would be a part of it if she could, he took exception to that. I don't know why she thought she'd win in this. She has none of the information that I have. None. He said that she would more than likely kill her own parents than listen to what she's being told to do. I never met her myself."

Warren sat back down hard. The man thought that his boss was going to walk away and also become president of the United States? He glanced over at Reed, who looked as if he'd come to the same conclusion. Nestor Carvey was insane. He might know a great deal about a great many people, but he was completely insane.

"You do know that this is going to get out, right? You know that as soon as people get wind of what you've told us, there isn't a snowball's chance in hell for him to get elected." Reed looked at Marshall before he looked back at Nestor and continued. "He's had people killed. Murdered for greed and money. Hell, he sold guns to the other side and our own troops were killed with them. No one will vote for him for that reason alone."

Nestor looked confused and shook his head. "That wouldn't be fair to hold it against a man who was only trying to make a living, now would it? I mean what if no one voted for you because you're young and stupid? Is it your fault that you're not out there trying to do the same thing that Jerry is doing? Well, I suppose that is, but you'll see. Once he kills this man…." Nestor pointed at Warren. "You'll see that he'll be a shoo-in for the White House and things will get back to normal."

"Take him to his cell." Warren hadn't realized he'd spoken out loud until Marshall moved to uncuff him and help him stand. He and Reed sat there for several minutes without speaking. He needed to go and check on Caitlynne, but was so overwhelmed by Nestor and his ideas about Jerry that he couldn't move. When Reed spoke he realized that he'd been working the entire time.

"There is just over eighty million in Garrett's account and almost half that in Nestor's. Freeman has just under a hundred million, and Small's is nearly triple that amount." He looked up from the screen. "I found Jackson's account. All the other accounts were in sequence so I…I found it."

Warren had to clear his throat three times before he could speak. "How much is in his? Or do I even want to know?"

"He has one point five billion."

CHAPTER SIXTEEN

Walker didn't look up from her face when he heard someone come into the room. He wasn't surprised by another visitor; they'd been coming in and out of the room since yesterday. When Khan sat down in the chair across from him on the other side of the bed, he didn't bother speaking to him. He didn't want anything to do with his brother right now, maybe not ever again.

"She kissed me."

Walker shifted on his chair and didn't look at Khan as he continued.

"She slipped something into my mouth and told me it was for me. I forgot about it until this morning."

Walker rubbed his thumb over Caitlynne's wrist and didn't speak. Khan apparently thought he had something to say he wanted to hear. When he reached out and stroked his finger over her arm, he put a small thumb drive on the bed between them.

"Roseann had taken pictures of us, remember? She'd also taken some video of us when we were shifting. When she left me that day she said she was going to expose us for what we were. She said that there would be nowhere for us to hide."

Walker looked up at him. "She never published the article. I looked for it daily, but she never did. Do you want to know why?"

"Caitlynne told her not to."

Khan shook his head.

"I don't really care, Khan. Get to the point and leave me alone with her. In the event you didn't notice, she's not waking up since she died saving your life."

"She stole it from her."

Walker looked up sharply.

"Lynne stole it all from her. There was a long video from Lynne telling me that I needed to get my act together and forget about the fucking bitch. Then she went on to tell me that she'd been watching Roseann and had discovered something about her. Something that only by chance did she find the reports about us."

"What had she been doing?"

Walker looked at Caitlynne when she took his hand. She looked at him with a huge smile, then at Khan. He'd never been so happy and relieved in his entire life. When he stood up and went to the bed with her, he'd hoped that Khan would leave, but when he stood up, Caitlynne stopped him. "I have to tell him what happened or he'll stand outside the fucking door and wait for us. You know how he is."

"I know that. Right now I could care less how he feels. All I care about is that you're awake and looking at me." He kissed her mouth gently. "Welcome back, baby. I love you very much."

"I love you, as well." He kissed her then, taking her mouth slowly in a long kiss. Lifting his head, he looked down at her and realized for as long as he lived he'd never see anything more beautiful than her right at that moment.

"Tell him. Tell him whatever he wants to know so that I can lay you back on this bed and hold you until I'm sure you're going to be all right." He settled in the bed next to her. "Khan, so help me if you don't go away after this I'm going to hunt you down and—" Caitlynne put her hand over his mouth as she spoke to Khan.

"She'd been working with someone high on the food chain for months, getting arms to our enemy overseas. The vice president would give her information on where the arms could be picked up, and she'd relay the information to the buyer. She was the courier as well. When the deal was over she'd take a large cut, and he and she would…celebrate in bed with the money spread under them like a blanket." Caitlynne picked up the thumb drive. "The papers are destroyed. Everything, including the videos she made. I made copies of everything in case I had to show the president when the time came. But it never came up again."

"So you knew about us before you came here."

She shook her head.

"Then how did you know to give this to Khan?"

"Your mom. She mentioned Roseann's name one day when I asked her about the poker up your ass about me. She didn't tell me a lot, but just mentioning the name made me remember the stuff I'd found." She handed the drive back to Khan. "You ready to know the rest, or arc you going to sit in a corner and be a big baby still?"

"You're not terribly nice, are you?" Khan frowned at her as he continued. "Tell me what you know about her. Is she dead?"

"Not that I know of, but that's going to change as soon as I find her. Right after Small was arrested she disappeared. I've heard that she was in Iraq, but not sure. She had made some pretty good friends while working against her government. I've been looking for her for some time, but not with much success. What happened to the president?"

"He's downstairs with my parents. He is enjoying himself, he said, for the first time in years. Did you know that he and Marshall were lovers?" Caitlynne nodded. "I figured you did. Is there anything that you don't know?"

She nodded, then looked over at Khan. "You didn't trust me. Even after I told you to sit tight and not move, you didn't trust that I would keep you safe. Why?"

Khan tried to stand, but she reached out and grabbed his hand. Walker watched his brother struggle, but didn't say anything. When Khan finally spoke, Walker could hear the pain in his voice.

"I had lost myself with Roseann. Not just myself, but my heart. And it wasn't because she was human…no, that's not right. It was because of her that I decided that no human was to be trusted again, because I couldn't trust myself. Especially with you."

Caitlynne laughed. "Why me, pray tell? I never did anything to you but make you pissed most of the time. I never once set out to harm any of you. In fact, if you remember correctly, you'll know that I told you all numerous times that I was going to leave, and when that didn't work, I tried to get you all to leave. You people are as stubborn as anyone I know."

"I doubt anyone is as stubborn as you are. And I know about you wanting no part of us." Khan looked at her with a sad face as he finished. "And, truthfully, I hated you because you were everything I wanted to be. Strong, honest, and you said just what you wanted. I found myself wanting to like you more than hate you…even though you were a human."

She shook her head and let go of his hand. "You do know that your own mate is going to be a human, don't you? The fates couldn't be nice enough to find you a nice pretty kitten to love. And she'll have her own set of claws too. But you'll not be able to turn her away. And you know what, Khan? I'm going to be right there beside you telling you with every breath I have that I told you so. And cheering her on as well."

"You know this how?"

Walker nearly laughed at the fear in his brother's voice.

"You have some sort of insider track on what's going to happen to us?"

"No. It's just me hoping. And when you do meet her? I'm going to hound you daily every time you screw up and piss her off. Because we both know…hell, Khan, everyone knows you're not going to be able to help yourself." She waved at him to leave. "Go on, Khan, close up your heart and hide away, but it won't do you a damned bit of good."

Khan left by backing toward the door, never taking his eyes off Caitlynne. It might have been funny if Walker didn't believe that she was correct in assuming that Khan would fall for a human. Walker just hoped she was strong enough to tame his brother and win his heart.

"You all right?"

He looked at her when she asked again.

"The reason I ask is when you picked me up at the scene, you were a bit pale. I didn't know if you'd been hurt or not."

"I'm fine. I wasn't hurt, but…." He crawled into the bed to be with her and hold her. "You terrified me when I saw you there bleeding so badly. And when Khan pulled your cat, I'd never seen anything more beautiful in my life. You're a very handsome panther."

She smacked his arm and laid her head on his chest. "It hurt. Will it always hurt like that?"

He thought for a moment she meant being shot, but realized she'd meant shifting. He loved it so much that he'd forgotten what it was like for someone to make you shift. His father had done the same to him when he'd been younger and had refused to shift because he didn't want to be different from the other boys.

"No. Just when you're pulled like Khan did to save you. When one of us shifts, it's sort of like the other self takes over and heals us quicker. If you are hurt as a cat, the same thing happens when you shift to human. No other species that I know of can do that. When you want to shift, it'll be a soft slow process that gives you time to adjust. When pulled, it's like an instant change and it hurts."

She laughed and started to play with the button on his shirt. "I suppose I should be grateful to him that he didn't let me die. He hates me that much, you know."

He thought about telling her that she didn't see the look on his brother's face when he came toward him. After her cat had lain in his arms Khan started to cry and beg her to forgive him. Walker wasn't sure if he'd ever seen Khan so terrified, not even when Roseann had threatened them all.

"I think Khan might have a different outlook on you. I think you might scare him a little. You are one mean bitch when you want to be." He hugged her when she laughed, and they both sat up when someone knocked on the door.

"Hello." His mom walked in after he'd answered the knock. He got up to take the tray from her and set it over Caitlynne's lap when she told him to.

"I can't possibly eat all of this." Caitlynne picked up a slice of ham and stuffed it in her mouth. "Okay, maybe I can. I'm suddenly starved. Thank you, Mrs. Bowen."

"It's Corrine or, if you'd like, Mom. Either is better than Mrs. Khan told me he thought you were hungry when he took off from here like he was in a room full of rockers and his tail was out. He mentioned that you were sort of scary."

"She told him that his mate was going to be a human and would give him a run for his life." Walker sat on the bed and took the last piece of ham. She'd made a huge dent in the amount of food in a short amount of time.

She asked him to go away. Well, she'd actually told him to go, but he smiled, kissed her, and left. His mom had given her some towels and some extra clothes of hers to wear. He would have loved to have joined her in the shower, but she said she needed some down time and she'd be with him very shortly. He left after another quick kiss.

Walker loved being in love.

~~~

Caitlynne made two phone calls before she got in the shower. She had an answer to one before she got out. Things were moving and now she just needed to talk to the president, then to Walker and the rest of the family.

She knew she had to be in DC for a while. Things in the office were going to be a mess for some time. There was no director and there was no one to see that things got going. She hoped that the president made a good choice. He'd inherited this group and could now start fresh. She was looking forward to the new guy.

Then there was the land. She'd overheard one of the brothers talking about the city trying to get them to sell and if they didn't, they were simply going to take it from them. She didn't want that to happen, and the call she was waiting on was hopefully going to fix that. She walked into the large living room to see that only the president and Marshall were there.

"Walker went to the hospital. Khan…he left. And I asked that the others leave so that I can have a long, nice chat with you." He gestured toward a chair. "Why don't you have a…you're not armed, are you?"
~~~

"Yes. Always. And I want to have a talk with you too. I'll go first." She wasn't sure how to take his laughter and decided to ignore it. For now, at least. "Did you know that the city council is taking the Bowen land because of some stupid park they want to put in?" He nodded, and she did sit. "Well, what the hell are you going to do about it? This land belongs to them and it will really piss me off if I have to come back here and kick some ass to make them understand that. I'm reasonably sure that I might even kick yours too."

"You were going somewhere?"

His question caught her off guard and she asked him what he said.

"You heard me. I asked if you were planning on leaving here. I mean, with Walker here, I just assumed that you'd sell your house in DC and come back here to bake cookies and have a few hundred kids. You're not?"

"I don't know what we're doing. I suppose the answer to that will have to do with Khan." She flushed and took the bottle of water that Marshall handed her. "Walker said he could be a doctor anywhere. He said he's got a very good reputation. And don't think I don't know what you're doing. I've used the same tactics on bad guys for a lot longer than you have. What's this have to do with this property, Mr. President?"

The president smiled. "Let's start this off right, shall we? Call me Warren. And I'll call you…what am I to call you?"

She flushed again. "Walker prefers Caitlynne, so I suppose that'll do. And I'm not comfortable calling you by your first name. You're my boss."

"So I am, but I would prefer that you called me Warren. Now. About this moving thing. I think that you will need to stay here. Khan and I have had a nice, long talk and—"

"*You* and Khan had a talk? What the hell do you mean you—?"

"Caitlynne, I may want you to call me by my first name, but as president, I would like to finish a sentence. Now, where was I?" He looked at Marshall who gave him a hint as to where he'd left off. "Yes. Now Khan and I have had a nice conversation, and he's thinking that having you around won't be so bad. I agreed with him. As for Walker being a good doctor? There isn't one better than him in all the state. All the country, I would say. But that has nothing to do with what I want."

He waited. She knew what he was doing. He wanted her to ask. Well, he could suck her big toe if that's what he wanted. She looked him in the eye and waited as well. She knew she was much better at this game; she'd had a bit more practice. When Marshall sighed, she knew he was going to break the silence.

"There's a position open now in the CIA. We wanted your help in filling it."

She looked at him then at the president.

"I'd be honored to help you interview potential directors. I can even do the background checks, as well as any other finding that you need." She was indeed honored. And surprised. She thought they would have a person or two lined up by now.

"No, none of that will be necessary. We know all we need to know about the person we have in mind. Brilliant, and damned good at their job. Mouthy, and a lot pushy, but a by-the-books type of person. No gray area for this person."

She was already looking forward to working with him. Caitlynne sat up higher in her chair and nodded. This was going to be better than she'd thought.

"So, will you do it?"

She looked at Warren, thinking she'd already answered that. "I said I'd help, but you just said you had someone picked out?" When they looked at one another, then back at her, she was more confused than ever. "Don't you? I mean, you do have someone picked out, right?"

Warren nodded. "You."

She was missing something. Looking behind her to see who they were talking about and seeing no one, she looked from man to man. It was the smiles that made her feel uncomfortable. Then it hit her.

"Oh no, no, no, no, no and fucking hell no." She stood so quickly that Marshall put his hand on his weapon and slid in front of Warren. "You can't be fucking serious. Me as director of the Central Intelligence Agency? Are you fucking nuts? I can barely organize a fucking grocery list, much less.... This isn't funny. Tell me who you really have in mind."

Warren, voice full of humor, told her he was not joking. "You'll need to clean up your vocabulary if you ever need to speak in front of the public. They might not get the idea of what you're trying to speak about if they have to bleep every other word. And I've had you in mind for this position since I took office."

"Why?" She sat down now, overwhelmed with what he was saying. "I don't understand why you'd pick me. I mean, I'm a pretty good agent, but this? What if I fuck up?"

"You probably will. Most of us do. But that's the wonderful thing about you; you have no problem with saying you've done so and give solutions on how you've fixed it. And another thing that I like about you is that if you need help you've no problem asking for it. Good traits in a leadership role." Warren took the file that Marshall held out to him. "There are other benefits to you coming to work for me. And they're all outlined here."

She took the folder and stared at it. Caitlynne decided that she'd rather be staring down a large group of people trying their best to kill her than this. She felt a small touch to her mind and nearly shied away from it. But when Khan spoke, she closed her eyes.

"You said you were okay with me staying with you guys because you knew that he was offering me this job and I wouldn't be here anyway, didn't you? How could you do this to—?"

"What job? I don't know what you're talking about. I felt your distress and wanted to…."

He was quiet, but she knew he was still there, a small touch of his mind to her let her know that.

"I deserve that. Your distrust of me and so much more. I can't tell you how sorry I am for you thinking that of me. And I will never forgive myself for the way that I treated you. But I will try, Lynne. I will with all my heart to have you forgive me."

"There's nothing to forgive if you really won't hold my being with your brother against him. He missed you terribly, and he would never forgive himself if he couldn't speak to you again."

Caitlynne leaned back in the chair and looked at the two men in front of her. They seemed to know that she was "talking" to someone else and spoke amongst themselves. She wondered if Walker could feel her terror when Khan spoke again.

"He can. He asked me to come to the house to see what the—and these are his words, not mine—what the fucktards are doing to you now. I'm right in the kitchen if you need me."

"They offered me a job. It will take me away a lot. I might have to stay in DC through the week." She wanted to talk to Walker in the worst way.

"Walker is delivering a baby right now and said to tell you he loves you. He said that you two can speak, but you have to stop blocking him. We think that the only reason you can hear me is because you're not able to block me out."

"I have to talk to Walker. I can do that…I'm sorry, Khan, that I thought the worst of you. I really am." She felt him hug her as if he were in the room with her. *"That was fucking weird."*

CHAPTER SEVENTEEN

Walker held the new baby in his hands and took a quick inventory of her. Ten fingers and ten toes. Pink skin and a loud, healthy scream. Yes, she was fine. Handing her off to the nurse beside him, he smiled at the new parents. Of course they didn't notice because they were too wrapped up in each other to see him, the man who had brought their little bundle into the world.

He didn't mind really. He loved this part of his job more than anything…bringing new life into the world to make it a better place. Walker sat back down and took care of the business of the mother, and was just about to check on the baby again when he felt the fusion of fear from Caitlynne.

"I don't…can you come to me?"

He nodded to his nurse and walked out of the room as Caitlynne continued.

"I'm afraid and I don't know what to do."

He reached blindly for the counter. If she was afraid then he was out of him mind with it. Trying to be as gentle as he could, he sent her his love and security and spoke to her without moving. He wasn't even sure that he could.

"What is it, love? Have you called Khan? He and the others can be there faster than I can. But I'm coming. Do you have your gun?"

"I can't carry it."

Christ, he thought, she was hurt badly if she couldn't hold her gun. He was pretty sure she slept with it under the pillow, but had never checked. *"I'm contacting my brothers. They can be there in—"*

"No," she screamed though his mind. *"Christ, don't fucking do that. I'm embarrassed enough as it is. Why I did this is beyond me. But I wanted to surprise you, and now look. I can't fucking take it back."*

Walker moved to the elevator, unsure what the hell was going on, but embarrassed he could handle a lot better than her being hurt again. He had been caring for her more than he'd been able to love her. He was ready to begin their life together.

When the doors opened he slipped inside and leaned against the walls as it took him to the lower levels and out of the hospital. He tried to reach her again, but all he hit was a wall of…not really fear now, but more of what she'd said. She was mortified about something. Reaching beyond that he had to stop again, this time right next to his car.

"Are you a cat, Caitlynne? Have you shifted?" He found he was grinning and couldn't control it. *"Did she just come over you or did you want her?"*

"How the fuck do I know? I was thinking about what it might look like and suddenly there I was, looking back at me with fucking fur. Why the fuck didn't anyone tell me how easy it was? You certainly didn't." He laughed. He simply couldn't help it.

"Are you going to laugh it up or tell me how to get back to the real me? You're gonna pay for this, you know that, don't you?"

He laughed harder.

"I mean it, Walker. I can't leave the house and I have this meeting thing with the president in a few hours."

"I'm coming to you now. Is there anyone in the house?" She told him no. *"Good, because you and I are going for a run when I get there, then I'm going to take you to the ground and fuck you so hard you'll never want to be a human again."*

He felt her arousal as if it were his own. He was glad he was sitting at a light because he was pretty sure he would have had an accident if he hadn't been. When she spoke to him this time it was without fear, without embarrassment of any kind.

"Will you chase me, Walker, if I run away?"

He adjusted his cock twice so it wouldn't hurt as badly as she continued to talk to him.

"Will you sink your teeth into me when you come like you always do? Will I come as hard as I do when you fuck me in the bed?"

He had to concentrate on driving the speed limit. He growled low when someone cut in front of him. If this kept up, if she kept it up, he was going to take her before they got to run.

"Be outside behind the house when I get there. And Caitlynne?"

She purred at him.

"You are going to come so hard that you'll be lucky that you can speak after this."

Walker pulled into his driveway just as a black cat streaked out the back door. He pulled off his shirt and was kicking off his shoes when he could smell her. She was aroused all right, and she knew it. Moving toward her, he took off his pants and let his cat take him. As soon as he shifted, he took off in the woods.

Flaring his nose, Walker went in search of his prey.

Her scent was everywhere. He should have known she would be good at hiding from him. Her experiences as a human would spill over into her cat as well. He loved hunting for her, and when he saw her again, his breath caught.

He'd seen her before as a cat. She'd been lying in Khan's arms and unconscious. She'd been bleeding too, her fur matted with it. He had picked her up then, and she'd looked at him for a second or two before slipping away again. By the time he'd gotten her home, she'd been human. He'd not asked her to shift again, because he knew she was nervous about it. Now he was glad that he hadn't. Seeing her like this made him glad that he was seeing her just as she should be seen. In the woods with all of nature surrounding her.

Her black fur was slick and molded to her body. Each line of her muscle and bone were defined perfectly. When she turned to look at him her eyes were the darker blue of her human ones, and bright with excitement.

Walker leapt after her. She was moving fast, playing with him. He wanted her to play, enjoy this version of herself. When he reached for her mind they connected on a level that had never happened to him before, and he sent her directions on where to go.

"I want to do this forever. Can we?"

He laughed at her question and told her they could more now that she wasn't afraid.

"I wasn't afraid so much as...well, I didn't want to fail. I didn't...I remember how much it had hurt me before and didn't want to scream like a little girl having her first cramp."

"You wouldn't have. I could have told you that if you'd asked." He had a feeling she might not have believed him and told her so.

"Oh, Walker, look."

He had guided her toward the waterfall at the back of their property. Each of the boys owned some of the original land, but he'd been lucky enough to be able to buy an additional four hundred acres at the back of his. Now he had just under five hundred of the most beautiful property in the state. He watched her go to the edge and drink from the lake that formed at the base of the falls, and he came up behind her.

He rubbed his body over hers and was rewarded with a loud purr. She reared her hind legs up and rubbed against him. When he started to mount her from behind, she slid from beneath him and into the water.

He loved the water in either form. More so in human, but his cat loved it as well. When she came above the water a few feet away from him he sat and watched her. She was swimming back to him when he stood up.

"I want you." He'd meant to be much more romantic about it, but he'd been patient long enough. *"Come here to me."*

Her cat snarled at him. He had expected that. She was as strong as her master and didn't like being ordered around. But he was bigger, much bigger than her, and he took her to the ground and laid over her as soon as she came out of the water fully.

Her scent nearly made him come all over her. When he bit into her shoulder to hold her still, she growled again. He felt his cock lengthen more when she tried to get away.

"Be still." She stilled immediately, but snarled again. *"I need to be inside of you right now. Fight me if you want, but I need this more than I need to breathe."*

His cock thickened more, incredibly more, when he was near her entrance. As soon as he entered her she pushed back against him. Biting her harder, he moved in and out of her, trying not to hurt her, but he needed to dominate her. Her blood filled his mouth as he pressed her to the ground. He moved slowly and nearly laughed when she told him to take her now.

Holding her down, he fucked her. He had had sex as a cat before with one of the local group's females, but never had he felt so connected, so overwhelmed with need. As soon as his balls began to tighten up he let go of her shoulder and came deep inside of her. Her own climax surprised him; females rarely came this way, but he should have known she'd be different. When he felt his cock fill again he pulled out of her and shifted.

"Come. Think of me fucking your human self and shift. I need to be inside of you again. Hurry." Her cat fell away and her nakedness nearly took him to the ground. He didn't even give her the time to stand or even to turn when he was behind her, his thick cock deep in her pussy.

She was slick with his cum and her arousal. He held her hips tightly as he plowed into her. His balls were soaked with her juices, and he knew that he wasn't going to be able to hold back once she fell over the edge again.

Her breasts swayed with each of his strokes, and Walker wanted to suckle at them. Pulling out again, he rolled her to her back, adjusting her legs on either side of him. Walker looked down at her spread before him like a feast.

"You have no idea how beautiful you are to me right now. You're so wet that I could drink from you for an hour and never get it all." She cupped her breasts and pinched her nipples. "That's it, baby. Make them pucker for me."

"Help me, Walker. Please. I want to feel you inside of me again. Help me come with you."

He stroked his cock and watched her.

"Walker, please?"

Guiding his cock to her heat, he leaned down, took one of her nipples into his mouth, and nipped. She rocked up and took him into her as she cried out his name. When her other breast was offered to him he took it as she wrapped her legs around his hips. Lifting his head from her, he watched her face as he moved to the pulsing beat of her sheath. She was as tight as he'd ever felt her.

Perfect, it was utterly perfect to see her this way. Every stroke of his cock changed her expression. He knew each time he touched her sweet spot. He knew the exact moment that she felt her climax racing toward completion, and he could see just when it took her, her face wondrously filled with rapture. His own climax grabbed him quickly, and he joined her, tumbling over the edge of a fall that had him wishing he would live forever just to be with her.

He lay over her. Walker wanted to lift her up, take her back to the lake, and bathe with her, but the thought of moving off her had him wishing he had napped before coming out to play. When she giggled, a sound he never thought to hear from her, he lifted his head to look at her.

"You're dead weight."

He moved then, thinking that he was hurting her.

"No, don't. Don't leave me yet. I love the feel of you like this. Warm after sex and breathing hard."

"Tell me if I get too heavy." She promised him she would, and she began stroking the back of his head. Walker closed his eyes for a moment. He knew he just needed a moment.

~~~

Caitlynne watched him sleep. She knew that she'd have to wake him soon because she had to go to DC with the president for a little while. She'd still made no decisions about the job because Walker had been so busy, but she knew that she should at least talk to him about it before she left. Her second phone call had come through. Touching his shoulder, he came awake slowly and reached for her as he smiled.

"No. If you pull me back to you, then we'll make love again and I'll be late. Not that I give two shits if I'm late, but he's done a few things for me, and I want to help him with this." She took a deep breath. "I have some money. A lot of it. And I've had it put into your account."

He frowned at her. "Why would you do that? I mean, I have plenty of my own, and if you think that—"

"I don't think anything. Shut up and listen." She flushed when he raised a brow at her. "Please let me finish. I was born to a wealthy family. My parents were rich, as were theirs. But they died when I was a kid, and…none of that matters right now. I inherited all of it, and because I've never had to touch it, the money I make working for the government has been just sitting there too. Now it has some use."

She started to pace and felt stupid doing it naked, then sat on a nearby log. It wasn't any more comfortable. She asked him if they could go back to his house.

They walked back holding hands, and she continued telling him about what she'd done. She could tell that each step that got them closer to his home, the more if felt as if he was moving away from her.
~~~

"The land deal with the city is finished. They won't be bothering you or your family about it again. The mayor said that he had someone banking on the deal, and his plan was to buy cheap or take it from you guys, then sell it to a developer that was slated to come to town in the coming months." Walker nodded, but didn't comment as they went into the house and up the stairs to the bedroom. "He's been arrested, as have a few members of his little group of assholes. They are in the jail, and your brother said he'd make sure that he stayed put. I believe him. If I had to bring someone in to help me, it would be your brother, Marc."

Walker still hadn't said anything. She'd hoped that he'd be okay with this, but she'd even take pissed. Some emotion would be better than none. She moved around the room and pulled one of his large shirts over her head. She'd have to bring more clothes from Washington. *If* he wanted her to return, that is.

"I'm going to go to DC with the president. He and Marshall are supposed to leave within the hour. I don't know when I'll be returning, but we can talk more if you want when I get back."

"No."

She looked at him, hurt that he didn't want to at least discuss this, and pulled her shirt over her head.

"I've said this to you before. Where you go, I go. I don't care if it's only for a week or ten years. If you go to DC, then I'm going as well."

"I don't think you understand. The president wants me to run—"

"I understood you. I heard every word out of your pretty little mouth. But I also remembered you saying that he had a job for me as well if we decided to live in DC through the week and come back here on weekends."

She moved to the bathroom, trying to not snap at him.

"Look at me, Caitlynne. Please?"

Without turning from the door, she poured her heart out to him. "I've already come between you and Khan. I won't come between you and your patients. They need you more than I do."

He came to her then, wrapped his arms around her, and held her. "But I need you more than they need me. I can't live without you, baby. I don't want to, not any longer. I love you very much, and I can tell that you want this job. I want you to have it. And can you imagine how great it will be on my resume that I was the president's own personal doctor? Damn, I'll be able to write my own ticket."

She laughed and turned in his arms. "Are you going with me now? I have to do something that I've been looking forward to for a long time. I get to tell Jerry that he's fucked and I'm going to take him down."

"Oh yeah, I'm going. And you're going to take me to your house there so I can tell you what we need to do to make it livable." She started to protest when he kissed her. "I might not have been in the house you had here but once, but you have the decorating skills of no one I've ever met. Have you ever heard of a houseplant, or even a photo? You had the most naked walls I'd ever seen."

She looked around his bedroom and could see what he meant. This room, like the rest of the house, was warm, inviting. There was family here in the pictures and things all about the rooms. Shells from a walk on the beach, pinecones from somewhere in the woods they'd just been in. There were pictures of all the men when they'd been boys. Pictures of the elder Bowens at their wedding. She nodded at him.

"Okay, I could use a picture or two there as well."

He snorted.

"Okay, then you are on your own. But the house in DC…it's not what you might be used to. I don't know when the last time it was decorated, but it had to have been at least fifteen years ago."

"Good. While you're kicking some ass I'll look around and see what we need. I don't suppose it's been dusted in a while, has it?"

She stuck her tongue out at him before answering. "As a matter of fact, there is live-in help. The house was my parents'. And for the record, there are a few things there that the staff cleans daily. Not a great deal, but a little. I got rid of most of it after I got into the Bureau. I was always afraid of becoming…becoming someone I'm not."

She kissed him quickly and turned on the shower. She had to threaten him three times when he tried to join her. They would never make it on time if he did, and they both knew it. She was just finished getting dressed when the doorbell rang. She went to answer it when Walker stepped out of his own shower.

The limo driver tipped his hat at her and nodded. "Hello, Miss McCray. The jet is ready to go, and the things you asked to be brought here are just there. Would you like for me to have them brought in?"

She nodded, and when Walker came down the stairs, three more people were there besides the driver. She introduced him to his new staff. "The week before I blew my house, they were living with me. But things had gone from bad to oh hell in a short amount of time and I sent them home. They've been waiting for me to call them back from DC for a week now. And I think that Dotty there took what little plants I'd let her keep in the house." He nodded. "I told you I came from money. I thought we'd have a little house built for them behind your house."

Soon, they were in the car riding to the airport. Walker hadn't said much until they got in the limo. He wanted to know how he was going to house them all, and what did they think they were going to do all day? She told him that they always did things for her and she loved not having to worry about the daily crap. He looked out the window as he continued.

"Anything else I should know before we get to the house in DC?"

She nodded as they entered the airport.

"Like what? Do you live in a mansion?"

"Yes. It had too many bedrooms and a bigger staff than the president has. Plus." She pointed to the plane. "That belongs to us as well." She knew if she lived to be a thousand years old she'd never forget the look on his face when he saw the jet. She was handed out of the limo by the driver. Then he reached in to help Walker out. As they walked up the steps and he stepped inside, he looked at her.

"How long do we have before we get there, and does this thing have a bed in it?"

CHAPTER EIGHTEEN

Jerry put his cell phone back in the mattress when he heard someone approach. He had been having problems with it for several hours now and was waiting to hear from Jackson again. The man was supposed to call him over five hours ago.

The cell door opened, and he looked up. Before now someone had simply shoved his tray of food under the door and left. The door opening this time startled him. He didn't bother standing when he saw who it was.

"Hello, Jerry. Long time no see."

Warren Russo did not deserve his respect, and he wasn't going to acknowledge it by answering him.

"I'm just going to have a…ah, there we go." A chair was brought for him by none other than Caitlynne McCray, the biggest pain in his ass since just before he'd killed off his own mother. She leaned against the open cell door and smiled at him. Jerry decided that when this was over he was going to cut her mouth from her face and piss on it.

"What the fuck are you doing still alive?" He didn't mean to say that out loud and was pissed when she laughed at him. He was going to have to learn to control his mouth. It had gotten him into more than a little trouble lately.

"Some days, I wonder the same thing. But I am alive and kicking, no thanks to you and Garrett." She stretched her arms over her head and he saw her badge and gun. The fucking cunt was pissing him off more.

"Get her out of here. If you want to talk, that's fine. Waste your breath, but I won't have her here mocking me." He glanced over at the phone when one went off. He knew his was on vibrate, but the sound had caught him off guard.

"The service has been cut off to yours."

He looked up at her when she spoke.

"We did that when your buddy, Nestor, told us he'd slipped one in here to you. He said to tell you 'hi,' by the way. He's been extremely helpful to us."

Nestor. He had wondered what had happened to the man. Garrett had told him once that the little man had more dirt on people than he had sense. Jerry looked away, thinking of all the information the shit had on him. The man had better not give up.... He looked at her again when she spoke. He asked her what she'd said.

"I said we have Jackson too. He isn't singing as much as Nestor did, but then we have enough on him to do what we want. He and you have been working together for a long while, and we now have all the notes that Nestor took to do yours and Garrett's bidding. It was very good of Nestor to do that, don't you think? By the way, his money with yours and the others will go a long way to helping a great many people."

If she had Jackson then she knew a great deal more than he'd been put in there for. He was not just going to be in prison for a long time now, but he was going to be put before a firing squad right along with Jackson and a great many other people. Jerry tried to wrap his mind around what was happening and only looked up at her when Warren stepped back into the cell. He'd stepped out to answer the phone.

"I don't know what you're talking about. And I certainly don't know any Marine named Jackson. You have me confused with someone else." When she threw back her head and laughed he tried to think what he'd said that had been that fucking funny.

"Oh Jerry, my boy, you are such a liar. That's really too bad too. If you had even tried to tell the truth, things might have gone a bit different." She kneeled down in front of him. "I never said he was a Marine."

He saw red. Nothing else at that moment mattered to him but to kill her…and he would too. Reaching for her, he felt his fingers move around her throat and he squeezed tightly. She was going to die and he was going to enjoy it.

But something moved…shifted, under his hands. Before he could let go he was holding onto nothing and she was…. Jerry couldn't move.

The large black panther had its jaws wrapped around his own throat and he was terrified. His bladder let go and he could smell the hot urine that was pooling under his hips. Something trickled down his neck and he knew it was his blood. Still, he didn't move anything but his eyes. He looked at Warren, who didn't seem the least bit surprised by any of this.

"You might want to be very still, Jerry. Caitlynne hasn't been a cat for very long, and I'm afraid she isn't used to her extra strength just yet."

Jerry looked at the cat who held him. Her eyes were as blue as the sea.

"I know what you're thinking. Caitlynne? No way. But I assure you, it's her. Isn't she beautiful? I don't think even the Bengals that I run with are as beautiful."

Jerry stared at him.

"Oh, did I forget to mention that? I'm a tiger. A rare white Bengal. My parents were very pleased when I was born."

Jerry felt Caitlynne's mouth tighten and he was sure she was laughing. He looked at her again and decided that he was dreaming. This would all be gone as soon as he woke up. He started to shift on the floor when the pain in his groin nearly had him jerk from her tight mouth.

"Careful there, honey. You don't want to claw his dick off. Though it might be preferable to what he has in store for him later." Warren stood up and scratched the cat behind the ear. "I'd ask her to shift, but when you tried to kill her instinct took over and she shifted. Her clothes, sadly, were not as lucky as you were in that she has some control over her cat. Clothing seems to be the least of your problems now, doesn't it? What do you say we have a little talk while Caitlynne here holds you until her husband shows up?"

Warren reached over and took the cell phone and then looked to his left, beyond where Jerry could see. Suddenly the phone rang, and Jerry just caught himself from reaching for it. Warren had turned it on to speaker after pushing a few buttons. It was Jackson.

"You motherfucking prick. When I get out of here, I'm going to hunt you down and cut your fucking head off. Do you have any idea how much money I'm losing by sitting here in this fucking jail cell? Millions. And you want to know something else? You're going to pay it all back to me." The phone went dead again.

"That was from earlier. It was a voicemail that we intercepted before his own phone was taken from him. He isn't any happier now than he was when he left this for you." He handed the phone to someone and sat back down. "Caitlynne, dear, your husband is here with your extra clothes. Why don't you go and change so that we can continue our conversation with Jerry? He will behave from now on, I'm positive of that."

The jaws released him and he still didn't take a deep breath. She stood over him, just watching him with her blue eyes. When her massive head leaned toward him again, he whimpered and flinched. Then she was gone.

"She'll be right back. So why don't you tell me what you know about the arms deal that you and Jackson had planned? We have some of the details, but not all."

He stared at Warren as if he'd never seen him before...which, from what he'd just learned, he hadn't, not really. He turned his head to the left and looked at the panther sitting there licking his lips. This one was nearly twice the size Caitlynne had been. Jerry looked back at Warren.

"That would be Caitlynne's husband. Mate, really. But it doesn't matter. He's going to be staying here helping with controlling you until we finish." Warren leaned forward slightly. "And he does have control over his cat and will not only rip your throat out if you so much as raise your voice to her, he will eat you for his dinner. I believe he would enjoy that, too, for all the problems you've caused his mate."

Jerry believed him. The cat yawned then settled down on his belly when Caitlynne walked in. She was wearing a pair of lounge pants and an oversized sweatshirt. He glanced over at the panther on the floor to assure himself that this hadn't been a dream.

He was pretty sure that the cat on the floor and the woman standing before him were as real as it got, and that by the time they left he was either going to be dinner for one of them or he was going to tell them everything they wanted to know. He didn't really have much choice in the matter now. He was a dead man either way he looked at it. He looked at the cat again and then at Caitlynne. She smiled and blew him a kiss. When he flinched from it he knew what he had to do.

"Jackson would set up the deals with all the men overseas and send the orders back to me. I had three men that worked for me that would do some creative ordering so that it never came back to us." Jerry continued talking until his throat was raw and even after when they brought him a bottle of water. He told them everything he knew. Everything.

~~~

Walker walked around the house. He had tried twice now to say something to Caitlynne, but frankly, he was overwhelmed. No, that wasn't right; he was freaked the fuck out. When they entered the fifth or sixth bedroom, he pressed her against the wall and covered his mouth with hers. It had the desired effect of shutting her up.

"You don't like it?"

He looked around the bedroom that looked like something from one of the rich and famous magazines that his mother was always bringing home from the store. "We can change anything you want. As I said, I think my mother had it decorated about a month or so before she died and I've not done much to it since."

He rested his head on hers. "Caitlynne, I know I asked you not to tell me, but now I have to know. Just how much are you worth?"

She cleared her throat once before answering and he knew it was far more than he had even guessed. When she pulled away from him and closed the door to the room, dismissing the man who had been following behind them, he sat down on the closest object. The chair looked much more comfortable than it actually was.

"I'm one of the richest...okay, you want the truth, don't you?"
~~~

He nodded.

"Even though you told me fifty times you didn't want to know?"

"Yes. I need to know. This house is not just a mansion and you know it. This house is big enough to house several large families and they'd never see each other. Not to mention there are several other houses in the back that I saw when we were in the last bedroom." He stood up and looked out the window. "Is that a pool, or have you had the ocean moved back there?"

"A pool. And don't be a shit, Walker. I tried all morning to tell you that the house was big. And so you know, those houses are for guests too. Not just the staff stays here." He turned to look at her and she flushed. "At last audit, I was worth just over five point five—"

"Five point five million dollars? Five point five—" He stopped when she shook her head. He moved to the big bed and sat. "Tell me."

"Five point five billion. And that's only in cash and houses. There are also the stocks and things that I have invested in that—" She stopped talking when he raised his hand.

"Who are you?" She turned away from him and he knew he'd hurt her. Standing again, he went to her and held her. She was stiff and unyielding in his arms.

"When they told me that my parents were dead I realized that I didn't know them. Not at all. I lived here with them for the most part, but didn't interact with them. They would bring me out during parties to show their pretty little girl off, then I'd be sent back to the nannies and maids. I lived here for another ten years with the people who worked for them, never knowing anything any different." She moved away from him and he let her. "The staff that came with me to Ohio had raised me, and when I explained to them that I was going to be living with you but had to travel to DC more, they said that they weren't leaving me. That you'd have to get used to them."

"I like having them there." He did too. For the first time since he'd moved in, his laundry was washed and put away and his refrigerator, which he hadn't even looked in for months, was full of things he loved.

"Most of the time we eat together when I'm home. They're the closest thing to family I've ever had." She knelt before him and took his hands. "I know that you've had a great deal thrown at you today. I'm sorry for that. I didn't want you to.... Walker, I don't know what I'd do if you left me."

He pulled her up for a kiss and then pulled her onto the bed. "I'm not leaving you. I can't. I love you. This house and the money are a lot. More than I ever thought it would be even when you told me that you came from money. I love you, Caitlynne. More than I ever dreamed possible, I love you. Besides, the alimony to you would kill me."

She rolled him to his back, straddled his hips, and sat up. He wanted to roll her to her back and take her again, but held her over him when she looked toward the windows. He waited for her to speak.

"I have something more to tell you. I don't want you to get pissed until I'm finished telling you, but it's important. Not just to your family, but to me as well." He nodded. "I've set up bank accounts for all your family. None of them will ever have to work again if they don't want to. The house, the one that your parents live in, and all the houses on the property are paid off, and the taxes have been paid in full for the next fifty years."

He swallowed hard. He knew that the taxes had been a struggle for his family. When they'd gotten the property they had agreed to pay the lien on it. Later they were told there were nine liens on it that amounted to hundreds of thousands of dollars.

"Thank you."

She nodded and continued. "I've also paid off all the debt of your student loans, as well as all the brothers. I had my accountant take care of it all. And even though the hospital has agreed to pay off your debt if you work for them another five years, that too has been taken care of, as well as a generous donation for them to break your contract so you can work for Warren."

He did roll her to her back then and settled between her legs. He stretched her hands above her head and was glad when she left them there. He started unbuttoning her blouse as he spoke. "While I appreciate you taking care of my family, you won't handle me again. Understand me?" When she started to speak, he covered her mouth with his hand. "I'm not finished. You won't do things like this without telling me first, and you will not be treating me as a kept man without letting me make some sort of payment arrangements for it." He lifted his hand from her mouth when she licked it. His cock jerked hard in his pants. He nodded his permission for her to speak, afraid if he tried to talk, he'd begin by begging her to let him take her.

"What sort of payment plan did you have in mind? I mean, I'm open to all sorts of suggestions. Like you could take out the trash. Peter, the cook, hates that job. Then there is the job of washing dishes. I know we have a dishwasher, but if you want to work off your...Christ."

He took her nipple into his mouth and bit on the tip gently. When she surged up off the bed toward him, he suckled as much as he could of the warm flesh into his mouth and held her there. When he lifted his head, he was breathing hard and wanting more.

"I was thinking I could be your sex slave. I could service you anytime you needed and be at your beck and call whenever you needed to come." He nuzzled her breast again and stilled when he caught her scent. "What do you think about children, Caitlynne? Do you want any?"

"So long as we're both here to raise them. So long as we make them a part of our lives and not a trophy to bring out and show off." She lifted her head and stared at him. "Why?"

"The reason I ask is because you're in heat. If we made love right now and over the next several days, you will get pregnant. Would you like that?" He nuzzled her throat and then licked along the pounding pulse. "Would you like to have a baby with me?"

She grabbed a handful of his hair and pulled his head up. The look in her eyes had him wishing he'd told her differently, had waited until they were home or at least somewhere more romantic than a spare bedroom in a house her parents had not loved her in.

"Are you serious? You want children with me?"

Carefully, he nodded.

"Will you let them come with us when we move between the two houses?"

"Yes. I wouldn't have it any other way. Besides, I think my parents would murder us in our sleep just to keep them if we did that." He waited for her to say something, anything. "Do you want to wait? You'll come into heat three times a year. We can wait until next year even if—"

She rolled him to his back again and tore his shirt from him. When she scooted back and tore at his pants, he stilled her with his hands. She grinned at him when she looked up.

"You said something about making love over the next few days to get me pregnant. We'd better get started before we miss the opportunity."

Laughing, he tore her clothes off her as well. At the rate they went at each other and clothes were ruined, he was pretty sure that, in the end, they'd be happy for all her money.

"As of yesterday morning it's our money. I had your name added to everything that has mine on it." She broke his zipper, pulling at it. "If you don't hurry, I'm going to start without you."

Well, he wasn't going to let that happen.

About the Author

Kathi Barton, author of the bestselling series Force of Nature, lives in Nashport, Ohio with her husband Paul. In addition to writing full time Kathi likes to spend time with her eight grandkids, three children and three children-in-laws. She writes to relax and have fun.

Her muse, a cross between Jimmy Stewart and Hugh Jackman brings them to life for her readers in a way that has them coming back time and again for more. Her favorite genre is paranormal romance with a great deal of spice. You can visit Kathi on line and drop her an email if you'd like. She loves hearing from her fans. aaronskiss@gmail.com.

Follow Kathi on her blog:
http://kathisbartonauthor.blogspot.com/

www.ingramcontent.com/pod-product-compliance
Lightning Source LLC
LaVergne TN
LVHW090938080826
845145LV00003B/792

* 9 7 8 1 9 3 9 8 6 5 2 2 9 *